good deed rain

Books by Allen Frost

Ohio Trio
Bowl of Water
Another Life
Home Recordings
The Mermaid Translation
The Selected Correspondence of Kenneth Patchen
The Wonderful Stupid Man
Saint Lemonade
Playground
Roosevelt
5 Novels
The Sylvan Moore Show
Town in a Cloud
A Flutter of Birds Passing Through Heaven:
    A Tribute to Robert Sund
At the Edge of America
Lake Erie Submarine
The Book of Ticks
I Can Only Imagine
The Orphanage of Abandoned Teenagers
Different Planet
Go with the Flow: A Tribute to Clyde Sanborn
Homeless Sutra
The Lake Walker
A Hundred Dreams Ago
Almost Animals
The Robotic Age
Kennedy
Fable
Elbows & Knees: Essays & Plays
The Last Paper Stars
Walt Amherst is Awake

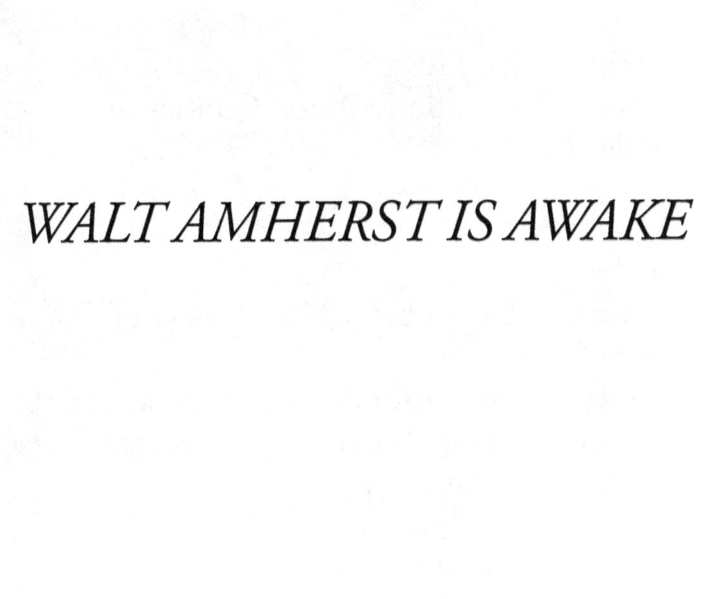
WALT AMHERST IS AWAKE

Walt Amherst is Awake © 2018
Allen Frost, Good Deed Rain
Bellingham, Washington
ISBN: 978-1-64467-466-6

Writing: Allen Frost
Cover & Illustrations: Aaron Gunderson
Apple: TFK!

Credits:
Variety, December 1945, Review of *White Pongo*.
Gene Autry, "The Girl I Left Behind," 1930.
Tom Robbins, "Bobo and His Keeper," *The Seattle Times*, June 24, 1962.
William J. Ehrheart, *The World's Most Famous Movie Ranch: The Story of Ray "Crash" Corrigan and Corriganville*, Ventura County Historical Society Quarterly v.43, no.1&2, 1999.

Movie Quotes:
The White Gorilla (1945)
White Pongo (1945).

WALT AMHERST IS AWAKE

Dreams, my love, are very mysterious things. They float around in the night air like little clouds, searching for sleeping people.

—Roald Dahl
Danny, the Champion of the World

INTRODUCTION:

Why is Walt Amherst trapped in a B-movie? And why *White Pongo*? There are many amazing, imaginative B-movies from the 1930s-40s, but *White Pongo* is not exactly the cream of the crop. Like any jungle explorer mindful of steps, what led me to it is a definite dream masterpiece—*Undersea Kingdom*, starring Crash Corrigan. That movie serial might be a sort of blueprint for this book.

It also sent me searching for a buried treasure. Somewhere stored away, I had an autographed photo of Crash that I found at Aladdin's antique store soon after we moved to Bellingham. Knowing more than me, that picture waited all this time (19 years!) to reappear on this book's back cover.

Mr. Corrigan wasn't only a cowboy though.

With his closet full of gorilla suits, Crash became the actor to hire anytime a sinister ape was needed in a film. And they made a lot of them back then; those inspiring old movies they reran on TV were crowded with gorillas.

So I did a little gorilla research. I remembered the famous Bobo who lived at the zoo in my childhood Seattle. Bobo died when I was 3, but he never went away. I always made sure to see his embalmed ghost whenever I went to the museum on class fieldtrips, or with family.

Gorillas and cowboys and a 1945 movie—I let all that and real life and dreams collide.

White Pongo never received much praise (at the time of its release, *Variety* panned it—see pages 52-53) but it couldn't have been all bad—it became the heart of this book. Truthfully, I didn't watch it more than a couple of times, so what do I remember about this movie? There's a fight scene filmed as gorilla ballet. Flowers planted on a trap door. And a great sequence where the hidden White Pongo is thrashing along beside the river, keeping up with the drifting canoes. Those are the details you look for in a movie like this. It does share with its peers, the utter freedom to explore anywhere in the imagination. That's the inspiration that led me to *Walt Amherst is Awake*. Writing this was an adventure in B-movie thinking, editing in stock footage from other realities and memories and letting story unfold like a dream.

Another reason to write this was to show where I am when I'm gone from home. Time at work flies me away from family and I thought this would maybe give them a glimpse of where I went without them. I had to create something out of all those hours lost—like Gene Autry in his serial *The Phantom Empire*, where if he didn't sing, he would lose everything.

Writing about work poses a challenge though. At its best, being there is like being in a zoo. I often catch myself daydreaming out the window, thinking how I'd much rather be walking to the water, down on the bay, following sidewalks, going wherever I wanted. Stuck in an office seems more like a sentence—and not the sort I like to write! So it took some effort to set a book there. But if I had to, why not treat it like a dream?

Usually I'm so tired out by the time night falls, I welcome the chance to sleep. I just fall into it until morning. Dreams become an escape, a cheap movie you can return to when you close your eyes, where sleep is another life and only a little bit away. Except for a few images, the exploration there is usually forgotten. With that in mind, this is an adventure of what dream state might be: a parallel world where our shadows are real.

—Allen Frost
Bellingham, Washington
Summer 2018

"When you leave the post, you go due north to the river then you follow the old elephant trail to the left. Well, just keep on going, you won't miss it… but…look out for the white gorilla."

—from *The White Gorilla*

At first the office was like any other day, 5 days a week, 8 AM-5 PM. At first, he thought it would stay that way, but that only lasted until he heard the girl tell him his stapler was gone.

"What?" His desk was covered with papers, strewn with pens and pencils, notebooks, receipts and gadgets. His hands ran across it all like a blind man in a tide pool. He felt the tape dispenser on the corner of his desk, but the stapler wasn't with it.

"She said she was just borrowing it," said the girl at the reception desk.

But Walt knew it was too late. He could see that plain as a movie he just walked in on. The part of the stapler was played by Ray "Crash" Corrigan and although he put up a valiant figure, throwing blows, breaking chairs and banisters, he was finally subdued and tossed in the back of a black sedan. The car roared off into the night, on a dusty road winding up the steep cliff overlooking town. A full moon perched in the clouds. The tires screeched, the music thrilled like a bucket of hornets. Walt wanted to reach over and open the door and push Crash out safely into the weeds on the side of the road. Crash could roll into a hiding spot in the roots of a tree. But all Walt could do was watch as the car took a last tight turn on the top of the hill, where it stopped next to a hole in the rocky cliff side. Inside the cave, they tied Crash to a chair and there wasn't a thing anyone could do to help.

Like someone surfacing from underwater, Walt Amherst took a deep breath and opened his eyes and moved to look at the clock.

Only an hour had gone by since he shut his eyes and his mind was still at work, replaying what happened with his stapler. It really did go missing for a while. How was he supposed to collate all his In-Box reports? They were stacking up. Finally, he had to go search the building, as if his stapler was some lost jungle treasure. That expedition took about ten minutes out of his day. He rubbed his eyes as he remembered and thought of how his dream turned all that drama into more. He couldn't believe the fate of a stapler took on so much importance in his life. Why was he led to believe everything happening at the office was so important? Deadlines, rules, worries and stress. He thought, "Why do I have to dream about work too? Isn't it enough for me to be there five days a week?" He rolled over and listened to the rain on the roof.

The rest of the night he was restless. He remembered waking up from time to time and looking at the clock, aware that sooner or later it would be 6 AM. There wasn't much to remember of his dreams in the morning. Most mornings he woke up and had no idea where he had been. It was like losing the memory of a past lifetime.

The room was dark as night but he had a feeling it was close to six o'clock. The alarm was set for 6:02 and after all these years he had trained himself to wake just before it went off. On the rare occasions he didn't, the buzzer would go off and it was a terrible way to start the day.

He raised his head off the pillow and took a look at the clock on the bedside table. The red digital numbers read 6:72.

His first thought was, "Oh no! I've slept in!"

He got up on his elbow and looked again. 6:72.

Finally, his brain began to rattle with those odd numbers. They weren't possible on a clock. Still, he left the blankets and his wife and stood, keeping bent so as not to run into the slanted ceiling which seemed lower today and pattering with rain.

He passed his son who slept in the loft, crept down the stairs by his daughter's door. She would sleep past noon if she didn't have school.

In the kitchen, Walt poured water in two pans—one for coffee, one for the tea he would bring in a thermos to work. He went through the usual routine. He could have done it in his sleep.

When it was ready, he took a cup of coffee into the other room and sat on the couch. There wasn't much time, less than an hour before the bus would be rolling up to the sidewalk and off he would go to the office for the day.

After his coffee, when he carried his thermos and bag and shut the backdoor, he saw something strange in the driveway. Wet from rain, the gravel shined like a riverbed and right in the middle of it sat a cat, orange and striped as a tiger.

When it heard Walt shut the gate, it stood up—it had been lying down, with its body tensed—then wings spread out from its fur. Before Walt could take another step, the cat shot into the air. It was fast. It was gone around the roof of the garage through a whisper of alder leaves.

That wasn't a cat Walt had seen before…the neighbor's had a gray one—once in a while, he saw it cross the lawn…but this one looked like a tiger and could fly.

A small sound, maybe two or three gravel stones, moved where the cat had been. Walt turned and noticed a bird flattened to the ground. It held its wings over its eyes and muttered squeaking like the hinge of an old pocket watch.

"You're okay now," Walt said. "That cat is gone."

The bird uncovered its face and Walt could see the black cap head. It was a chickadee, one of his favorite birds. When he walked on the wooded path, he loved to listen to them and sometimes he would whistle to them and they would pop along the eaves of the house and answer him.

This one was very close. It straightened up, tucked its wings back and said, "I have something for you." It spoke to Walt but it kept looking nervously back and forth, up and down the driveway. Pivoting slightly, Walt could see something shiny that it hid. "I'm lucky you came along when you did." Its voice was somewhere between a chirp and a teakettle whistle.

"What's going on?" Walt said.

The bird hopped aside and pecked at the sparkling button shape. Then, just as quick, it covered the thing with its wing. "I don't want that cat to get it."

Walt bent near. Whatever it was, couldn't he just pick it up and hold it safely in his hand? The bird gave a couple hops to the side and let him do that. Walt decided it was more than an ordinary marble pushed into the gravel, but that's what it looked like. Just before he touched it, he thought how it looked like a round piece of the rain. Silver colors seemed to rush around in it.

It happened so fast—there was no slow bus ride in the rain up the hill, past trees and the muddy chocolate paths that led from the sidewalk into the woods where the homeless camped—all of a sudden he was back in the office. It happened so fast it was just a blink and another day on the calendar began.

The aqueduct that ran along the ceiling was leaking. Papers spiraled down like falling leaves, some landing in the In-Box tray on Walt's desk, others scattered over the floor, or hit buckets set to catch them. A lobster scuttled to a crack in the wall, carrying a page in its claw. Walt hoped it wasn't important. There were so many receipts and invoices to keep track of. He set his bag and thermos beside his desk and sat down. "Let the games begin," he said.

And no sooner had he sat down than he was on a wooden bench between the hulls of a rowboat. In each hand he held an oar. The little boat creaked forward with each stroke. The land and the town stuck on grew distant behind him. He saw a rumbling train, no bigger than a toy, travel along the shore. A seal broke the mirrored sky, exhaled and looked around.

There were many days at work he wished he could leave his desk and without a word to anyone, hurry down the hall, out the door, onto the asphalt, and just keep going towards the bay. He was so close to it he could see the water every day. There were dark green islands and boats on it. The urge was in him to go to the shore, to the docks, where they rented kayaks and those little rowboats that floated like paper hats. So much time can be lost while not doing what you really want to do. It was so simple too, pulling oars through the water, smelling the sea, breathing it sharp and real as the breeze in a cemetery. No sounds of office machines or people needing this and that. The only ones around him would be gulls, the seals, and the fish below. Maybe a heron might pass by, flapping like a telephone book, slow enough to look for words typed on its wings. But he couldn't hold onto that vision—the oars in his hands were replaced by yellow pencils, one in each hand—and a desktop covered in paper.

There was so much for him to do and more orders were raining down on him from the faulty aqueduct. First, maybe he should call Work Control and let them know about that leaky thing. How could he get a single job done if more kept falling on him from above? He shook an invoice off the phone and dialed extension 3420.

"Good morning, Work Control."

"Hello, this is Walt Amherst in the studio office. We're having trouble with a leaking aqueduct."

"Okay, I'll have to transfer you to the Workflow Overflow Department."

"Thanks."

There was a click in the receiver pressed to his ear. Something pattered and squeaked and Walt couldn't help it—he pictured a creature fluttering madly through the dark. His call became a bat, let loose in a pitch black night. It was calculating its blind way with a sonar that made pictures in its head. There were clock towers, steeples, trees, alleys with fire escapes and those bright delicious flowers that danced in its mind—moths!

Walt had seen enough. He hung up the phone. He didn't need to float in the night. He had places to go and things to see.

He left the phone booth and got on the bus. It didn't matter where it was going. He walked by the driver and found a seat beside someone pretty. That wasn't all, she was familiar; they knew each other from somewhere. He knew she carried a violin case that hid a Tommy gun. She and Walt held up banks, insurance peddlers and factory foremen, dealers and salesmen, frauds and bureaucrats and anyone who wasn't a friend to the poor. It was easy to find villains—they masqueraded right in plain sight. It was enough to turn you outlaw. Walt and the girl became Dillinger and Pretty Boy Floyd. Songs were written about them—not the kind that played on the radio—Walt heard them around fires, boxcars, in barns, brick walled rooms with candles and lofts. They were folk heroes, but finally he and the girl were trapped. There were police all around. Walt could feel the end of their song. But he let time slow for just a second. The bullets hovered in the air like bees. He turned her into a shadow and hid her safe on the wallpaper behind a door, where they would never see her, so her memory would be a mystery. The magic disappearance of her was painted like the quiet that hangs in the air when the music is over.

A long way from office rooms and paperwork and all those oh-so important tasks that don't amount to the dust on the wing of a fly, a telephone rang. It was a warm day; the kitchen window was open. Walt could see outside. On a green wooly lawn, a clothesline was hung with the things an old cowboy would wear. There were other trailers parked around on their own little plots of land, a cedar fence that was falling down, an oak tree and sunshine. A bird feeder and a blue plastic wading pool.

It was a place Walt knew about but he wasn't quite there, he was only visiting, he was caught at the window while a telephone rang. He stirred in his sleep. Maybe it was downstairs? A midnight call that came and went, a mystery that left you wondering.

One time long ago, Walt and his wife were out in the woods at the edge of the city. They left her blue toy car parked by the road and followed a path. The branches and leaves quickly bunched about them as if to hide them from danger. It felt like one of those old jungle films where the forest was some magic other world. Once you entered, there was music and animals were everywhere.

This really did happen already, Walt thought, I'm remembering this, though it seemed covered in soft down and cobwebs. They climbed the steep path and at the top of the hill behind them, through the trees, they could see the city. Huge, wide highways raced with cars, bridges, towers, factories, stacks of concrete metal and sharp glass. It looked like a different planet seen through the trees. It was like the wrong window had been put on a wall.

Walt's wife pulled his sleeve, "Look, it's this way." She stepped around the yellow NO TRESPASSING tape strung between trees. One of the trees had a sign nailed onto it like a painting:

BY ORDER OF CITY ORDINANCE

The woods got smaller the way they do on an eye chart. Walt kept getting the feeling this was a memory repeating. He and his wife had been married for twenty years, but now they were young again and those were the days in so many ways. As soon as they were past all the warning signs and tape, as soon as they were among the trees again—the city at their back and fading away—they began to look around with the wonder of astronauts.

She said, "Look!" and pointed at a Douglas fir. Walt laughed. Eight feet up its trunk, it had a face, crafted perfectly from moss and clay and bark. A content look bent the corners of its mouth and its eyes were shut like a Buddha. There was more…a treehouse that was delicate as a wooden lotus, a bus with turrets and skirled with moss. How did it even get up here in the woods? How had any of these handmade houses and cartoon constructions appeared? The people living here were artists and they had built this place among the trees as if the city on the other side of the hill and all its laws and rules didn't exist. But that was the trouble: the city was real and it wanted them out. They had already sent men with clipboards and cameras and yellow hardhats. Soon it would be bulldozers. Being here, looking around, seeing how different, it was like holding your breath in an undersea kingdom. You could tell it was only a matter of time before they would lose everything.

"You can stay here!" someone urged them,

"We need more people like you." He showed them a treehouse. It would have been perfect a thousand years ago. But you could tell it had been left in a hurry. A woman's scarf was caught on the ladder. Walt thought it looked like something his wife would wear, as if they had already been here and had to become refugees in the face of some nightmare. He didn't even have time to grab her hand or hold her in his arms before he was in a hurry again. It was just one of those things—you were in one place, then you were in another.

Down the driveway, turn to the right, Walt
pedaled. It wasn't raining so he cycled. Work
wasn't that far away, just follow the road. It
was a river you got in and it would take you
past windows, gardens, deer staring from trees,
a squirrel in a housedress watching from her
nest, up hills, around corners until you were
there.

Walt got off the seat of the unicycle and
rested it against the bicycle rack, no need for
a lock, nobody would go riding off on it but
him. Outside the circus, very few could. He
may have sighed a little heading for the doors.
It helped to whistle, to make a song out of it.
Another day in the office.

It also helped to imagine he didn't know

what would be awaiting. What if his desk had grown legs like a rhinoceros? What if the walls had sprouted leaves and the room had the dimensions of an African jungle? A village by the river, with canoes pulled onto the bank like sunning alligators and the tent where he typed keeping time with the drumming.

Inside, at his desk, reimbursement forms had to be filled in, signed and filed. Permits, supply orders and parking for elephants. First off, the script needed edits. A copy was left by his typewriter, a stack of paper labeled *White Pongo Goes West* with a handwritten note: <u>see changes, Act V</u>. He cleared the orange peels off his desk and sat down.

The door of the hut shook open as one of the set decorators burst in. "I need you to order more palm leaves," she said. "These ones are all damaged." She dropped the faulty stack of them on the floor next to his desk.

Walt said, "Okay." He had his eye on the orangutan who had just shuffled in. That one was always trouble, but there was more. A flash of movement crossing the window warned him the director was on the way.

Sam Newfield entered the room like a broken shutter bang—they all did; they were all so important—and he flew straight at Walt's desk. "Listen up. Have you seen the changes to Act V?" Smoking a cigarette like a steam engine, Sam sat on a box of live ammunition. "It's where Pongo is on the train—I want some better dialog there, I want some spark, some chemistry, I want *My Little Chickadee*. I want that gorilla to be W.C Fields and Mae West all rolled into one."

"Okay," Walt said.

With a loud thud, the orangutan had knocked a can of paint onto the floor. The thick yellow pool of it oozed around the corner of Walt's desk.

"Oh God," he groaned and shut his eyes.

The jungle was gone. That was a relief. For a moment Walt thought he was in the arctic. The landscape and the sky above were an almost blinding white. In the middle distance, a locomotive train was stopped. It looked like the train drawn in a children's book, one that had used all its coal to huff and puff to this desolate spot. There was nothing to hear but the breathing of the wind and it was cold. All that white snow. Walt tried to rub his arms warm. Or was it very hot? He couldn't tell. It was a black and white film he was watching; he didn't know if he was surrounded by snow or sand.

A gorilla crawled out of the train. Pongo's white fur suit was a stark contrast to the iron wheels and dark cars. This must be Act V, Walt realized. We're in the desert of the Wild West. That means it must be warm.

The gorilla swung his arms like a windmill then loped towards the front of the train and the endless seeming desert ahead. Walt was glad to see Crash Corrigan had a better role since playing the stapler. He was rising in the ranks. What a good lope he had. Walt hoped Sam was getting it all on film, but there was no sign of the director, cast or crew and only the sound of the dry desert wind.

When the white gorilla was beyond the train, it nearly vanished in the blank expanse. Pongo was probably dying for a glass of water, Walt thought. He was too. How long had they been out here without water? The desert blew cold across him and Walt rolled and woke up.

He was freezing! His wife had pulled the blankets over onto her side. He had a vision of snow. Is that what he had been dreaming? He was also thirsty though. He didn't look at the clock as he got up—he didn't want to know. It still must be in the middle of the night sometime. He held out an arm and touched the wall in the dark as he made his way to the stairs. No wonder he had been dreaming of snow. He rubbed his hands together as he reached the ground floor, the kitchen and made his shadowy way to the sink.

Running fingers across the counter, Walt found a cup. The curtains above the sink allowed some murky light. How could he get so thirsty dreaming of snow? He wondered what else was going on. It was funny how fast dreams disappeared. They were only made of sand.

As he finished drinking, he listened to the clock tick above the stove. It was too dark to read the gray round face of it. It was no friend of his. That clock would be hurrying him along in the morning, before he rushed out the door to the bus.

Walt set his empty cup back on the counter and retraced his steps across well-worn shadows, back up the stairs. His son was asleep in his bed under the eaves and as Walt entered their bedroom, he saw the shape of his wife with the blankets pulled over her. It was cold. He supposed his breath could be seen like a steam engine.

Getting back in bed, he retrieved what

covers he could and lay there staring at the shadows, thinking about sleep. Why do people go to sleep? Because they're tired—yes—but also because there's another world they can explore. It isn't a known place either, it changes every time you go. Like a sort of miraculous airport, all you had to do was shut your eyes.

That's what Walt did. He knew it wouldn't take long to be there.

He was right.

Sometimes he would have to toss and turn a long while trying to leave this world.

Not this time.

That bird, that chickadee, was waiting for him. Walt noticed it in the tree on the corner but he was in a hurry. He was late for work.

It was dusk and the streetlights were lit on Main, and the glow showed in the trees like dandelions. He saw a streetcar and the old automobiles with faces like owls. Walt was someone else, in another time. He was skidding on the sidewalk past storefronts, a grocer's bin full of apples; he was all elbows and knees like James Stewart running through Bedford Falls. This place had that look. People were lined under the theater marquee, already buying tickets and going in.

Walt must have done this before, flown in late and thrown on his red buttoned usher's uniform and found his mark by the right hand door, smiling and welcoming and letting people in. The seats were filling. It must have been a Friday night the way they were all piling in, talking and laughing and watching that big blue curtain ripple. All these years through a broken economy and a horrible war, the curtain had been opening to other worlds. Fred Astaire and Ginger Rogers had danced in here, Buster Keaton and the Marx Brothers appeared, William Powell and Myrna Loy, Veronica Lake, mysteries, monsters, and detectives. A great train of stars had been and gone. More were always waiting for the houselights to dim and the projector to roll and clack out a new river of light. Imagine the whole country, little towns and cities, connecting to that light. You could hypnotize the whole country if the story was right.

Across all the chairs, on the other side of the theater, Walt saw Rita Jane. He knew her name. That was about all. But how he dreamed of her…Then, when he tried to talk to her, he turned into Henry Fonda, bumbling on words about the weather.

The projectionist told him it would be okay. Up in that bottled room filled with zeppelin machinery, spinning film reels, and the echo of actors and music, he told Walt, "Usherettes really do make the best companions, as long as you don't mind the smell of popcorn."

Wouldn't it be nice to take her hand and walk into the next black and white background while the orchestra played?

"Walt!"

A hand clapped down on his shoulder and Walt gave a jump. "Mr. Newfield!"

His manager seemed to steam with cigarette smoke. "You were late again."

"Yes, sir, I'm sorry." He stared across the room, all gold and lit like the Titanic, for a last look at Rita Jane.

He must have known her in a different life, back when movies were like that.

Goodbye.

Walt was lucky they had office jobs everywhere. There were dishwashing jobs too. There was always something he could do.

The morning steps to the art studio were brightly slicked with rain. The bricks were made of unexpected shapes, animals, faces, and words. A raven cawed from somewhere in the sky. Walt didn't have time to look for it. He even forgot for the moment that he could fly. He passed the unicycle parked by the door and hurried into the building.

Just inside the doorway was a cube with a TV screen on each of the four sides and an endless loop of *White Pongo* film. It just showed him from the back, his shoulders and head, as he walked through the jungle. Also the sound of his feet, snapping through the underbrush. It went on and on endlessly. Was it an artistic statement or a social criticism meant to convey the drudgery of the day to day? It was art, so who knows? The title card next to it gave it a name: Accidental Ecclesiastes #4.

And just in case anyone was tempted to step in there and turn the channel, the TV was roped off and a sign warned:

ELECTRICAL SHOCK HAZARD. PLEASE DO NOT ENTER.

He must have tripped on time—he found he was already at his desk. There didn't seem to be a reason for him to be wearing a gorilla suit, but he was.

Walt couldn't see much through the eyes in the mask, but he caught glimpses of others wearing ape suits too. They acted like contestants on some awful television show. Some of them were hamming it up worse than the real White Pongo ever did, waving arms and yelling temper tantrums. Not Walt. He sat at his desk the same as always. He could have been doing his job. "How about that?" he thought, "I've been replaced by a gorilla."

His boss, Mr. Newfield, stopped next to Walt and handed him a note.

Dear Mr. Amherst,

I am writing to thank you for submitting yourself to the application procedure. Unfortunately, the review committee did not accept you.

The review committee is faced with making difficult decisions during this appraisal because of the large number of qualified applicants as well as the limitations of space. To ensure that applicants can successfully complete the program in a timely fashion, the number of entrants must be balanced with the number finishing the program.

You are welcome to resubmit yourself to the next review.

We appreciate your interest in our program and wish you the very best.

> *Sincerely,*
> *Sam Newfield*
> *Director & Committee Chair*

Mr. Newfield moved around the room passing out those slips of paper. Walt watched the reactions. He saw one ape fall on the floor and throw a fit. A few of them brushed their eyes or held each other piteously. When Newfield and his crew were done delivering bad news, they started to tell the winners. You see this sort of thing everywhere. Who was Newfield and his committee to judge? What did they really know about White Pongo?

Walt was glad to wake from that dream. For

just a second, there was a split in worlds, then he was back asleep again, right where he left off.

The paperwork in the room had grown tall into towers and a perfect paper replica of the Brooklyn Bridge loomed beside him. It stretched from his desk, over to the desk on the other side of the room. Traffic crossed it, little cars, taxis, buses and trucks, and dreamers no bigger than dots would stop by the guardrail to stare at the sights.

The woman at the desk across from him asked, "How was your weekend?"

Walt stopped looking at the fine print on his hands and said, "How was my weekend? Yesterday, a sick dog came staggering up our street, all shaggy, hot and snapping and gasping for air. Foaming at the mouth."

She listened to him blankly.

"So I got my rifle. I had to remove my eyeglasses to take aim at the sick beast." He aimed an imaginary gun and shook his head miserably, "I had to shoot it."

"That sounds a lot like Atticus Finch," she said.

He laughed. She guessed right.

The bridge shook and a cloud of pigeons fell

off. The tiny blue scraps landed on the big stack of envelopes like a flock of birds on the roof of a barn.

Walt had a hundred or so submissions. They would take him a full day to go through. "How many did you get?"

She said, "148. How about you?"

He shook his head in doubt; he had no idea. He would find out. Raising his arms like an orchestra conductor he said, "Let the games begin."

Twice a year, the studio put an ad in the *Herald*.

You are in Demand!
You Can Draw!
Make money with your brush & pen!
If you love to draw, paint, or sketch
If you have hidden talent
DRAW WHITE PONGO!
You may win an Art Scholarship
and acceptance to a prestigious
Art Studio

A committee of artists would judge the entries. Walt had to process them, make spreadsheets, charts and notify all the applicants once the results were in.

Honestly, a monkey could do his job.

White Pongo could do it, if he wasn't lost wandering in the Wild West.

Walt liked all the different Draw Pongo entries. Some of them were inspired. A painting of Pongo holding a guitar. Pongo walking with a herd of buffalo. Everything had something to do with Pongo out west. As Walt sorted the pictures, they became a movie…Pongo leaving the city by train, through the hobo jungles where he sat on the roof of a boxcar and sang. The land leveled out along the sea then the train climbed into mountains. When they came down into the plains, there was nothing but miles of yellow rolling hills with the occasional ghost town or haunted mansion gone to seed. In a slowed down canyon, the train was stopped by a gang on horseback. They took everything they wanted, including White Pongo, and returned to their ranch, the starlight and another campfire song. Pongo would either have to escape or join them. Walt turned the next page. This was a weathered looking poster:

WANTED

Train Robbery, Escape
White Pongo

Age: Unknown
Height: 6' 2"
Weight: 350 pounds
Build: Muscular
Hair: White
Eyes: Red
Marks and Scars: Probably

If you are in possession of any information concerning the whereabouts of White Pongo contact the authorities immediately.

It fluttered on a telegraph pole in the prairie wind.

That's as far as the movie went.

It ended when the office door opened with such a gust that it shook the Brooklyn Bridge. Paper fell like playing cards.

"The window in Room 252 isn't working!" Anyone else might not have believed the sight of her, but Walt was used to it. A huge chicken quivered in front of his desk. She held her squawking head tucked beneath her wing. It had fallen off again. That happened every time she got excited. Often, in other words. "The window!" the big hen repeated. "I can't teach my class when it's not working!"

Calm is the best way to talk to a chicken with its head cut off. Walt stood. "I'll see what I can do."

She flapped and juggled her head. It almost fell to the floor as she screwed it back on.

Upstairs, he opened the door to the studio and went in. Everyone had a desk and everyone was busy drawing White Pongo. As Walt walked along behind them, each picture moved slightly forward as Pongo, in cowboy boots and ten-gallon hat, pushed open the door of a saloon. By the time Walt got to the end of the row, the animated gorilla had stepped through the swinging doors. The last girl in the row drew Pongo's sharpened smile.

It wasn't difficult to spot the broken studio window. The wall full of windowpanes faced the dark forested hill. The green was streaked with rain. A cold winter river flowed across them, except for one section that stood alone. It wasn't broken though—if anywhere was broken, it was the office he worked in—the window was a yellow, sunlit view of a pleasant world, tall red hills, chaparral, pine and a blue sky, watercolored on.

Walt knew where it was. He had been there in movies and television. It was the vast ranch-land of Corriganville.

Walt took a step closer to the light and warmth. That was so easy he took another.

He was in a parking lot surrounded by 1950s and 1960s cars, the kind of chrome and shape he only saw in old photographs. Ahead of him, across the gravel he saw a frontier town where horses were tied before the storefront and saloon. Birds were singing in an oak tree and up in the air the big Corriganville sign was tipping, coming down. A crew in overalls were trying not to drop it from their ladders. The birds were still singing fine as the words came down, but Walt knew the scenery was changing.

He was a bit surprised to find he was dressed as a movie cowboy, but he supposed it made sense seeing where he was. He fit right in. "What's going on?" Walt said.

The Corriganville sign hit the hard packed dirt with a metallic clang. The hired men caught their breath now that the sign was parked on the ground like a station wagon. "The ranch has a new owner," one of the men told Walt. He pointed to a big red truck. Tucked in the bed was the new owner's sign, fresh paint, neon trim with lightbulbs that would pop at night. The fresh letters spelled out: HOPETOWN.

Walt remembered where he was—it was 1965 and Bob Hope bought all that land that had once been other planets, Fort Apache, the thundering plains of the Lone Ranger and Tonto, Sky King, Gene Autry, and even the set of Robin Hood's Sherwood Forest. Now it belonged to Pale Face, alias Son of Pale Face, alias the Lemon Drop Kid. How could it happen? What about all that history? Where would the old Western stars go to live out their last twilight years? It couldn't end like this, with the Wild West thrown at the wind.

Walt crossed the dusty parking lot and climbed the wooden porch in front of the country store. An old broken stuntman sat in a rocking chair, pulled into the shade. Walt put a coin in the phone on the wall and dialed.

"Yeah," he said when the operator answered, "I want to talk to Bob Hope."

"Just a moment, sir."

The old fellow in the chair stirred.

It got quiet on the line as Walt waited for that famous voice. He was surrounded by sunshine, fresh air and the beautiful hills and he was ready to fight to keep them that way.

"How do you do? This is Bob 'One-Foot-Out-the-Door' Hope telling you to make it snappy or my shoes will do the talking.”

Walt laughed. He couldn’t help himself. He thought of all those *On the Road* movies and the radio show he loved.

“Hello?” Bob continued. “I know you’re there, I can hear the meter running.”

Walt could hear it too, but why was he dressed as a cowboy on a ranch set, talking on a pay telephone to Bob Hope? Wasn’t Bob Hope dead? Thinking that ‘I’ve been asleep and you’re just something I dreamed about’ tried to ruin everything and for a moment it almost did. Then he remembered, he wanted to tell Bob Hope something important. “Mr. Hope, I just wanted to ask you about Hopetown. I see the sign going up now. I wanted you to know that there’s a lot of us cowboys that have come to think of this place as our home—we’ve been here for a while and I hope you won’t throw us all away.”

Walt was pleased he got to say it, though he didn’t know if his words got through. He was rolling over in sleep and the scene was brushed with a fresh coat of paint, setting him on a jade colored sea.

An oar plashed in and left a swirl. Walt was rowing back to work. Sometimes a swell would take him up and turn him like a dial so he would have to correct his direction. His destination was a black barge. It floated offshore like an old shoe and could have been easily overlooked if it wasn't for the sound it made. Not that you could hear the ship itself, not from the shore with the waves and the gulls and the clanking lines of sailboat rigging in the harbor. All the sounds of the town too would fill your ears with cars and trains and birds and planes and whatever else was happening on the land. But if you had a radio, then that block of black wood out there was sending you a signal.

The next time Walt turned to look over his shoulder, he could see the barge quite clearly. The tall radio tower on it spiked the air like a flower. He was a long way from shore and he knew if he stopped rowing and leaned over the hull he would look down into that deep colored water and start to see strange creatures swimming by. Some of them had sharp teeth, some of them were long as school buses and used to chase him in his dreams when he was young. He didn't want to think of those nightmares. There was probably still some old moth-eaten shark looking for him.

Another swell brought him with a scratch

against the splintery wooden wall of the radio ship. He waited for the next rising wave to lift him so he could step out of the rowboat and onto the deck.

Right away he noticed a lot more animals on board than usual. But that could easily be explained by the music piping out of the horn-shaped air vent cowl. There was straw on the deck by the studio door and a yellow hen sat on top a barrel. *Dilly's Hillbilly Radio Hour* was in full swing. A brown cow and a sheep stood beside the lifeboat.

Walt passed the studio and entered the next doorway. Banjo, guitar and a steady thumping bass echoed about in the hall. He saw what looked like an armadillo scurry away. Walt went into a room no bigger than a closet and sat down at a desk. The chair creaked with his weight like a spoken hello. The desk had been waiting for him. It had nothing else to do but grow paper like thistles, crabgrass or deadly nightshade. One of Dilly's hungry goats could have a field day in here.

He reached for a wooden speaker on the corner of his table. Beside the typewriter, it wasn't much larger than wren's birdhouse. He twisted a dial and heard the fading end of some Appalachian song. As it warbled away down the other side of a mountain, the station chimes tolled. It was the start of the next program.

"Songs of the Black Capped Chickadee," came the voice off a crackling record, followed by that bird's familiar call. That song was one of Walt's favorites. If birds were in jukeboxes you could play for three minutes, this was Walt's choice. He often listened to this program— *Common Birds of the United States*—while he worked, and it was possible he made this request. He remembered walking in the woods not long ago when the chickadees were singing up in the leaves like small record players. They poured out a short high reedy whistle then tipped back, refilled and sang again. Walt listened to them call to each other from tree to tree. They moved around too, like pinball marbles or the signal on a radio. Funny, the station was playing for the birds. He wondered if there were chickadees tuning in, crystal sets humming in nests, antennas strung to the heights of their trees. For three minutes, they stared into some distance in the air, listening to that bird, famous to them as Bing Crosby. Maybe it brought back feelings of first learning to fly, leaving the nest, finding love or losing love, something only a chickadee could know. At the end of the record, when the Eastern Phoebe came on, they turned the radio channel.

"White Pongo" is the story of a safari's long trek through the Belgian Congo in search of a white gorilla supposed to be the missing link. With action revolving around a band of extras dressed in monkey suits who snort, beat their breasts and act just like Hollywood extras dressed in monkey suits, the film is a drawn-out affair.

Plot strains credulity all the way; with stock shots of jungle beasts having no bearing on the story thrown in at random. In the middle of the jungle, the safari guide and several of his riflemen mutiny, kidnap the daughter of the British scientist who heads the expedition, and leave the rest of the party stranded without supplies while they set off to find a fabulous gold field. White gorilla then follows the mutineers, strangles the guide and takes the gal off to his jungle cave. He gets into a poorly-staged fight with a black gorilla just as the stranded party, who have followed, arrive in the nick. As the albino dashes his adversary over a cliff, the riflemen wound him with two shots and put him in a cage to take him back alive to England, where the scientist hopes to prove he is the missing link.

Excepting Richard Fraser and Maris Wrixon in the leads, both of whom deserve better treatment, rest of the cast constitute some of the most wooden-faced actors seen on the screen. Faltering direction keeps the action to a snail's pace and a better job of editing would have helped things. Film editor, however, probably didn't have much to work with in the first place.

Walt took the train back to land. It made more sense than rowing. The tracks were laid on water and the train slid across with a hiss. The spray made rainbows in the windows. Why was he doing all this work, going back and forth? It was all for a family he only saw for a few hours in the evening, who knew him only as someone who came home tired, when he just wanted to lie down and be carried away by old black and white movies.

That reminded him of White Pongo and a scene he had thought about before came to life.

One early afternoon in 1945, the radio was talking about the destruction of Europe and Japan. Ships were sinking on all the seas and skies were falling with burning planes and bombs, when Crash Corrigan carried his heavy gorilla suit into the bathroom of his apartment.

He tossed it in the bathtub. It looked like a deflated ape. All the African air had gone out of it. Crash opened the window above the tub all the way, pushing the curtain aside. If Los Angeles wanted to look in, feel free. They were about to see Crash pour four big bottles of bleach over his famous gorilla suit. He wore rubber dishwashing gloves and one of his desperado handkerchiefs tied around his face. Crash had been promised a good role in two back to back pictures—*The White Gorilla* and *White Pongo*—but they needed a snowy gorilla.

A dance band played on the radio as he began to turn his tub into a bleach pond. He coughed through the checkered cloth and his eyes teared up as he held on tight to the gorilla skin. It would be a miracle if the fumes didn't knock him out cold.

Walt supposed that change did bring Crash something new to work with—the white gorilla became a stranger to its fellows, there would be long drawn-out fights whenever they met. He was feared or despised by everyone in the jungle and hunted by Americans.

He stepped off the train at the harbor, into the peaty smell of low tide. The river ran under the pier and carved towards the sea. A salmon or two came and went. A few gulls loitered on the driftwood by the mud.

The train that dropped Walt off had gone winding back out to the islands.

He tricked himself looking at the sky. He had a brief feeling that he was in another world. The sky in his dream was alive as a goldfish bowl. Strange flying machines darted above him, some of them airplanes resembling lawn-mowers. He could often see a pilot holding on for dear life. Something with stripes like a bee clattered over the roof of the cannery and Walt was left looking at a telephone pole. Stapled scraps of paper decorated it, most of them torn so only corners remained, or just strips with words that fluttered.

Walt was drawn forward down the cobblestones to read the handmade poster calling him.

MISSING
Name: White Pongo
A white gorilla gone missing on 2/17 at night.
He is very friendly, 43 years old.
Call 559-5551. REWARD!!

He didn't want to think of poor White Pongo lost in the city. Where would he go for shelter, how would he survive? Walt thought of him all alone, climbing a fire escape to the top of the *Herald* building where he would sit in the hot red light of those neon letters watching the bay for a steamboat back to Africa.

That was when the Marshmallow Girl

appeared. It's so nice to have someone to hold hands with. He remembered when his wife used to do that, out of the blue. He didn't know anything about this girl who held his hand. He couldn't have described her or picked her out of a crowd once she was gone. He only really knew her from the soft touch of her hand and the feeling she gave him. She reminded him of that Everly Brothers song and he thought of her as a sort of angel—he had an idea she would be waiting for him when he left the living world, to lead him beyond. That's what she did now, holding his hand, as if he had gone balloon-like, effortlessly pulling him a foot off the ground, taking him away. He knew he had to be somewhere. He was in a cloud, going through a tree, a billboard, a parked car, past a dog who watched him from a porch. Her hand fit snugly around his fingers as they floated across a park into the early morning sprinklers without getting wet. She was talking to him too, but the whole world was all one sound like the tone of a beautiful bell. He never wanted to let go but when she did, he was left standing in an alley beside a screen door.

Walt didn't always work in offices of course. For a long while, he washed the dishes in different city kitchens. This was one of those places, he could hear the dishwashing machine whirring and a radio going. He knew this place, the kitchen, sink clatter, the smell of the chlorine and steam.

He could step right back in if he had to and with the Marshmallow Girl gone, he guessed he would have to. It wasn't the heaven he hoped for, opening the screen door and going in. A shift of tubbing dishes, glasses, silverware, scrubbing big soup pots and pans, stocking the shelves again with plates so hot and clean they took the prints off your fingertips.

The washing machine gave a clunk as its cycle ended so he lifted the metal door and let all the steam pile out like a boiling cloud. With it clearing, Walt saw someone forming and in a second he recognized who.

The familiar dishwasher was so intent he didn't notice Walt as he set a heavy tub of dirty dishes next to the sink. There was some piano song on the kitchen radio and Walt wanted to say something to Robert Kennedy but what?

Robert reached an arm into the dishwashing machine and pushed the clean tray out on its rollers through to the other side. Then he lifted the empty tray from the sink and started to fill it with the plates, bowls, cups and glasses from the tub. Grabbing a handful of knives and forks and spoons, gathered like silver bunches of flowers, Kennedy's eyes were steady, jaw set and it was clear as ever he was efficient at this job.

Whether it's really happening or not, you can often see famous people in dreams. Once Walt met Jack Benny, a couple of times he had seen Sylvan Moore. The dream with Jack Benny was an old B-movie scene. The soldiers of Unga Khan were locking him in the Transforming Machine, telling him, "No harm will come to you. The rays will merely transform your mind so you will no longer interfere with our plans." Jack carried his violin in. He was framed in the window by surrounding steam and flashing light. All Walt could do was watch as Jack Benny left for the next world.

Walt watched the fog pour out the opened dishwashing machine while RFK put in the next load, played in time like ballet to the tinny radio on the shelf.

Finally, Walt said, "I don't know if you get the news in here," he glanced at the transistor playing some big band song, "but we could really use your help again."

Robert Kennedy smiled and quickly became serious again. "I have quite a lot to do where I am." He pulled the silver door down again and restarted the machine. There was a heavy crash of water inside, the rattle of porcelain and glass, a loud storm going on. "Excuse me," he told Walt with another quick look as he stepped around Walt to gather the plastic dish tray waiting on the other side. He was a shepherd to the never-ending flow of that herd going through the wash.

Walt backed towards the screen door. He didn't know what it would take to bring Bobby Kennedy back. Walt watched him make a stack of plates and pick them up, holding them close to his apron the way you would carry a tired child and he didn't say anything more as he left Walt at the door. Kennedy's eyes said it all, hurt by something deep in blue water, they darted at Walt and looked away. Was he even Robert Kennedy, Walt wondered, or just another wounded young man? Walt couldn't tell, he could only fall away, out the door, into a thick gorilla suit.

His feet slapped on the cement walkway behind his office building, past the steam plant, through the billowing white clouds that seeped from its seams. Walt couldn't see much through the eyes in the mask and it was like breathing into a pillow.

He was following White Pongo to the woods, onto the mossy wet wooden stairs that led up into the ferns with trees all around. Walt's gorilla suit wasn't so loose on him now and it was easier to see. As far as he could tell, he could turn his head and the forest was everywhere.

White Pongo loped along, moving fallen branches aside. Walt had to run to keep up with him. A loud blue jay hopped the spiral turns up a tree. Walt liked being in here much more than a room with walls and windows. Only a train, far in the distance, told him he wasn't really deep in some hidden jungle.

The white gorilla stopped in a clearing and sat like a patch of sunlight on the ground. A tent was hunched in the brush, clothes dried on a rope tied between two trees and stones were piled in a circle around the black remains of a fire. Some kindling and branches were stacked next to it.

This wasn't how Walt expected White Pongo would be living. Then again, what would he want with crowded Beverly Hills, expensive cars and a guitar shaped swimming pool? Why trade away the birds and quiet nights in the trees?

Pongo scratched at a spot on the packed dirt. He swept it with his broom-sized hand and motioned for Walt to come over and look.

A square was outlined on the ground. Walt was no longer a gorilla, though he didn't seem to notice the change, that he wore shoes and clothes instead of fur. He knelt beside what he could now tell was a hatch. He pressed his fingers into the groove and pulled the lid.

It was funny. It wasn't what he expected. In the midst of all this forest, below them was a ladder leading down into shadows and coppery light tangled as the mechanical engine room of a submarine. It reminded him of the Transforming Machine. He didn't want to go in. If he had any sense he would have wished himself out of there. Sometimes he could do that. It took a special presence of mind to remember we have that power. He knew if he wasn't careful, he could become part of the clockwork and wasteful of what it meant to be alive.

From his desk, Walt had a statue's view of the clock on the office wall. He could have built a bridge to it, through the air, with pilgrims going back and forth, bringing the news. It's 10:23, it's 11:07, it's time for lunch… And in the afternoon, the caravans would have been dragging, carrying the time: it's 2:14, it's 2:58, it's 3:01…4:30. Long days looking at the clock were making him half robot. There were circuits connecting him to that plastic face and slow moving hands.

That reminded him of the woman at the post office. He stood in her line for years, buying stamps for envelopes and packages. The last time he saw her, she told him she was ready to retire this upcoming April or May. "No more getting up early!" she laughed, "No more of this room. I can do whatever I want to!" She added, "The first thing I'm going to do is throw my alarm clock out the window!" He could see that happen. He watched it tumble like an acorn to where it cracked on the cement below. Not a sound would come from it anymore. "How about you?" she asked Walt. "When do you get out?"

"Soon, I hope."

The telephone rang on his desk and his hand sprang to answer it.

"My daughter didn't get accepted into the program," began the sad radio song. For every artist who passed the Draw Pongo guidelines, there were those who did not. He kept their submissions in other thick folders. A cabinet drawer was filled with them. There were White Pongos in there that the daylight was never meant to see. They were in shadowy sideshow tents set up beside the circus. Walt had to keep them itemized and organized and out of ordinary view. He had to admit, there were more wonders in that locked cabinet than ever crawled along the walls of the studio.

Why did there have to be a judging eye anyway? Walt thought about that every day. Wasn't it enough that someone chose art to be their path in life? Shouldn't they follow it and see where it goes? Good for them if they lived in lopsided rooms, roofs that would turn into wings, streets made of water, windmill girls and colors that would flow like a tide. It would be a different world.

They were safe there.

Walt cared for them like the zookeeper on an island off the edge of any map, far out at sea.

Where the ocean is wide, with nothing but horizon on any side, a freighter left the sight of Africa. It was 1945 and the sea was still littered with shipwreck and crashed airplanes. Lines of ghosts walked on black oil spills. Mines still floated and torpedoes, almost out of breath, looked for one last target. The ship crawled through it carefully. Down in the cargo hold, White Pongo steadily beat the bars of his cage.

England was another day or more away and Sir Harry Bragdon sat at a desk in his room, preparing his notes for the Royal Society of Explorers. What a triumph this would be for him, returning to the gray bombed-out capital with mankind's missing link. It was the find of the century! White Pongo, that magnificent white gorilla, was proof that man had left the jungle horrors to create civilization, beauty and art.

The ship crept on, scratching a wake, leaving a charcoal pleat in the air. The endless thumping of the caged gorilla beating in time with the propeller carried throughout the ship and through the water. It ticked like an alarm clock left on a sunken ship. The person who winded it and set it on the shelf would never wake up.

Sir Harry only heard the clack of his typewriter, everything else was background noise. He wrote about the imprisoned beast down below who was so close to human, only one small step from reason and emotion. There was still so much he didn't know. What if they gave him a grant to write more?

Floors below, White Pongo was remembering his far-off home, and his sad fate when all he did was admire Maris Wrixon, carry her to his cave, get locked in a fight with another gorilla he knew, get shot by a hunter, stuck in a cage and put on the waves. By the time they reached the English Channel, the beating heart echo had nearly stopped.

Wearily, White Pongo opened his eyes. He was slumped in his bamboo cage, planted in an English drawing room, beside a wall lined with portraits. A table full of scientists were gathered nearby, still and serious, just like those oil paintings on the walls.

"This is the key to the most amazing anthropological discovery of the century," Sir Bragdon explained. He pointed at the gorilla and continued, "Here, my friends, is the unmistakable proof of the existence of the missing link between man and monkey."

"*Ape*," someone muttered, "not monkey."

And another voice interrupted, "What basis do you have for calling him the missing link?"

Morgan Freeman gave the explorer a disapproving look. "Don't tell me it's because he's white."

"Gentlemen!" Sir Harry said, "I am convinced that he is! A strange beast of simian characteristics, but with the faculty of almost human celebration." His voice shook, "In the few tests we've been able to make, he has shown a much higher intelligence quotient than any other ape we've ever heard of."

"We too have had some time to observe this animal," Morgan Freeman said from the head of the long table, "and it appears to us that you have discovered nothing, more or less, than a very sad, white gorilla."

"Quite right, quite right," said another scientist. Walt recognized him as the actor who played Watson in those old Sherlock Holmes movies. Walt liked to imagine there was a casting room full of actors just waiting to step into their scene in dreams.

And oh no, how like Dr. Frankenstein Sir Harry Bragdon felt…rejected by the scientific community, bounced back to his cold hotel room with Pongo, a ball of melted snow.

"We'll show them," he told the gorilla. "We'll go where you will be understood for the miracle you are." Another ship, another long ocean voyage, across the miles to America and further from Africa.

That's another story.

If you weren't happy with the ending of *White Pongo*, seeing him shot, captured and hauled away in chains, it was only natural to wish for another story. Here is how it went.

White Pongo Goes West was only a dream but it seemed just as real as being awake watching it.

Without family or friends, unknown in the new world, Harry Bragdon and his gorilla struggled to survive. Stock footage of high-rise Manhattan, busy streets full of traffic, soup kitchen lines and boarding houses, hotels that rent by the day and the twirling lights of a carnival by night.

The once renowned jungle explorer and his amazing discovery found work in a pitch-penny sideshow act. Bragdon would bring them in as the barker, White Pongo would set up the pins.

"Step right up, don't be afraid! This is a two-for-one show! The thrill of a lifetime! Not only do you get a chance to win a prize, you get to see the world's only white gorilla in action! It's a show you won't see anywhere else on the planet! White Pongo!"

Walt got the feeling it wouldn't last. You knew that sooner or later Bragdon would lose Pongo in a poker game, or a circus would make an offer Harry couldn't refuse, or maybe the gorilla would sneak out of the trailer some night and hop a passing train. He would watch the world from the boxcar door and wait for all signs of man to disappear.

A train was passing. That sound could slip easily into your dreams.

Dragging a cloud of black coal like a tattered shroud, it rattled and shook through the 1865 towns, carrying the coffin of Abraham Lincoln. Later, in 1968, it was Robert Kennedy on the same tracks. Wherever it went from New York to Washington D.C. and beyond, the whole countryside would stop and it was so sad Walt could barely keep going with it. Sometimes that railroad sound would wake him from his sleep. The trains were just far enough away from their house that the mournful cry would stir against the window and start the coyotes howling.

How did Sir Harry Bragdon feel about the way his gorilla disappeared? He couldn't help thinking about it. He had gone to the Congo and stolen a rare creature from the jungle, shot, caged and carried it across oceans to another world for what? When science and intellect failed, it became some sideshow attraction. Then Harry went and blew it all, selling off White Pongo to the circus for cash in the hand. The money didn't last. It was gone before he knew it. He was right back where he started.

Were people born into some coin-operated machine? Was he winning or failing? He watched White Pongo make it to the silver screen. Then it was over.

What happened to that poor gorilla? It ended up in a zoo.

There had to be a way to make amends. If he could make things better, he would.

One day he saw the answer in a comic book:

OWN A REAL TEXAS RANCH

Own a mini-ranch in Texas—one inch square. We'll send you a legal deed and a map showing where your ranch is located. Send $1 to TEXAS RANCH, Amarillo, Texas 79108.

Harry saved what he could. He put a dollar aside whenever he could. He thought of that poor gorilla, hopes dropping further and further. If he could save enough to buy a good sized portion of land, maybe White Pongo could return to a sunlit world like he used to know. His new territory was marked in lines. It took Harry a year, but he finally bought some land. Somewhere out near Amarillo, there were toothpicks pushed an inch at a time into the sand.

All it needed was a gorilla.

And a lot of rain.

Walt floated in the wake, turned over in the air above the railroad tracks and tumbled onto the earth.

He was half in a field of tall yellow weeds with his legs stretched onto the cut grass of somebody's lawn. It was sunny and warm and birds were singing. He saw laundry on the line, cowboy clothes, and faded letters painted on the rusting metal side of a familiar trailer—*The Crash Corrigan Show*. The words looked old as well-worn clothes, hung out to dry on a beautiful day.

As Walt watched, a man opened the door of the trailer and stepped outside. He held the door for a friend. Both of the men were in their 70s and they wore cowboy hats and boots that clunked on the two metal steps to the ground.

Walt wished someone would turn the volume up. He could barely hear their conversation, lost in the birds around him. There was also a train going by somewhere out past the field.

Walt didn't have any trouble recognizing the two cowboy stars. He knew them from movies and TV. It was Crash Corrigan and Gene Autry. As he pulled himself forward, he heard a little of what they said. They laughed a lot. It reminded him of the way his grandfather and best friend would talk on summer afternoons. They both had cigarettes going. The smoke crept around them like rope.

Suddenly Gene held up his wrist and stared at the watch. Walt could hear the panic in his voice clear as day. "Listen, Crash," he said, "We've just got time to get back to the ranch before the broadcast. If we miss it, we lose the contract and Radio Ranch!"

"Don't worry, Gene," Crash said, "I'll get you there."

"Where's my horse?" Gene panicked, looking about the yard. "Where's Champion?" There was sunlight and a robin with a worm.

"I'll get you there," Crash repeated. "We'll take my car."

It was a pale yellow station wagon, with wood paneling and tires that squealed on the tar as they left the trailer park. In the backseat, Walt rocked like a bowling pin. This was exciting. Things were like a movie, a Saturday matinee in 1936, and Walt had a front row seat.

Crash drove like a true maniac, taking corners on two wheels, running red lights, passing cars and swerving around a truck with only inches to spare. "Whereabouts is the Radio

Ranch?"

"Just up ahead," Gene pointed. "Things sure look different though. A lot's changed around here."

"Yeah, well that's progress." Crash avoided a city bus and screeched into an alley, knocking garbage cans aside.

"That's the place!" Gene cried. "With only a minute to spare!"

Their station wagon bumped across the last street into a parking lot and stopped. A herd of those big heavy shining cars and pickups they make nowadays gathered around them as the two old men leaped from their doors. Gene had a guitar in one hand and moved swiftly to the center of the asphalt where a microphone stand was waiting. He was just in time.

"Radio Ranch is on the air. This is Gene Autry offering another broadcast. Today I'm going to sing 'That Silver Haired Daddy of Mine,' a request, but first a song about a broken heart." White Stetson, kerchief, black embroidered shirt and guitar in hand, he stood there like he used to with the Radio Riders behind him, long before the hazy background was parking lot, fences, glass buildings and billboards.

I close my eyes and dream of one
The one I love so dear
And now I am old and lonely too
I'd love to have her near

A parking lot attendant stared out the open shuttered window of his little booth. His hand rested on the telephone, but he forgot all about calling the police as he listened.

The girl I left behind
Is a girl I'd like to find
With her rosy cheeks and her curly hair
Her eyes are blue
And her face so fair

There's a scene in *White Pongo* where the beast scares Pamela half to death. She faints dead away and he touches her golden hair. That was nine minutes before he got shot in the chest.

I wonder does she wait
Down by the old front gate

Where we kissed goodbye
She said you're mine
The girl I left behind

Gene Autry turned into clouds as he began to yodel. The sound was fragile and sad. The lot attendant dabbed his eyes with a handkerchief. White Pongo watched from the corner of an alley behind a castle of pallets. His chin dropped to his silver fur; he seemed broken as King Kong.

The girl I left behind
Is a girl I'd like to find
With her rosy cheeks and her curly hair
Her eyes are blue
And her face so fair

When Gene started to yodel again, trees appeared, shimmering. The acrid smell of the city was gone, replaced by pine, sagebrush and ranch sunlight with a creek trickling by. Gene Autry was able to take them back into some other dream and push aside the Phantom

Empire for a little while.

"Walt!"

He jumped. He had been leaning against the soft wallpaper, watching the movie, and you weren't supposed to do that. The manager had crept up on him.

"Follow me," Mr. Newfield hissed.

Walt was caught in the cloud of cigarette smoke as he trailed behind, up the theater aisle and out curtains to the lobby.

Newfield stopped at a plain looking door and told Walt, "You need to go to the basement and find the last reel of film."

Oh no, Walt thought. He knew what this would turn into—he had been there in nightmares before.

"And be quick about it, Walt. The projectionist needs it."

"Okay," Walt sighed. "Okay, I'll hurry."

The door opened by itself and he was halfway down the steep wooden steps. The shadows of a thousand monster movies hung from the joists. Any one of them could have dropped onto him.

The basement light came from a torch like glow here and there on the walls, although further back the cement foundation turned into caverns and who knew how far that went and what lurked and shuffled in that dark. Under the city were miles of abandoned coalmines. They stretched everywhere and sometimes they collided with old buildings like the theater. Air vents chiseled up into backyards. If you got close to one, you could hear it breathe.

Walt wanted to be quick—he didn't have any trouble with Mr. Newfield's order—all he had to do was find that last can of film and he would run back upstairs. But it was hard to tell shadows from solid objects. Everything seemed to be part of the same darkness and nothing wanted to be found. Was there a spinning wheel left in a corner filling the room with black? Other props that once stood in the lobby were stacked around—cardboard palm trees, James Cagney's gangster silhouette, boxes, costumes, poster rolls and tools, carpentry scraps and the hundred other shapes of forgotten days.

Most of all, Walt tried not to think of the ghost. It was impossible not to. If you found yourself down here, that was the first thing that haunted your mind: The Ghost of White Pongo…It was rumored there were paintings made by the suffering gorilla, canvases worth millions of dollars by now. Everyone who worked at the theater had stories, remembered times something rushed in the dark, or made a map fall, or even worse—heard the heavy footsteps cross the cellar floor.

A long way from the stairway, Walt told himself if it happens, if White Pongo leaps out at me, I just hope to get it over with quickly.

Walt tried to make a joke of it once when he was talking to Rita Jane about the weather.

She was cold and held her arms crossed. She didn't believe in stories of the supernatural, but he asked her, "So you don't think that a ghost in the basement would affect the temperature in the rest of the building?"

Oh yes, White Pongo was waiting for him, only a few feet away, where the shadows leaned around a pillar, but more King Kong than that was a childhood memory that stopped Walt in his tracks.

In those pulp comic books he liked to read in his room many moons ago, there were ads for 3-D glasses, joy buzzers, black gum, a toy box full of everything you needed to start a war, and best of all, was the ad for the life-size White Pongo.

6 FEET TALL IN AUTHENTIC COLOR FOR ONLY $1

Just imagine your friend's shock when they walk into your room and see White Pongo BIG as life, as awful and sinister as any wild dream. A full 6 feet tall in chilling full color on durable 80 pound stock, and so lifelike you'll probably find yourself talking to him. Won't you be surprised if he answers? Just send $1 plus 25¢ to cover postage and handling. Money back if not satisfactorily horrified.

He read that by flashlight, moonlight, lamplight, and the lazy sun of Saturday afternoons. What would happen if he ordered it? Would the mailman knock on the door with a box big as a casket? Would he have to help carry it upstairs to Walt's room? Would there be lightning in the window when Walt ran scissors along the taped seams and tore it open? What would it be like having his very own White Pongo? Some part of him never let him find out, never filled out the envelope and sealed it with a dollar twenty five. It was a mystery that stayed that way while he grew older and other things became more important.

There was no reason to imagine it would reappear here, so far from the days of pulp comic books, taped to a thick pillar in the basement of a movie theater. Walt gave a jump and yelped.

It was White Pongo in faded full color on a six foot scroll of yellowy paper. SO this is what he would have got in the mail? A long rolled up piece of paper to put on his wall. He always believed it would be the creature himself, White Pongo, who would be delivered. That was so mean to target kids that way. An adult would know better—there's no way a dollar could make a monster appear.

Walt touched the crackly surface of the poster. There was no fur or form. He supposed this scary image stuck in the dim light was the source of the ghost. Anybody coming down here would see that and run upstairs and the legend would grow. *The Ghost of White Pongo…* What a title. Too bad they never made that movie. It would have been perfect for today's market—a tortured circus gorilla left for dead in the catacombs beneath the stage. A beautiful young woman and a brave usher are sent to retrieve the last roll of film and they get locked in, lost among the furnace pipes, chains and violent shadows. Walt thought of Rita Jane and wouldn't it be great if they were able to calm that poor beast and send its ghost off to a shimmering resting place? They would find the can of film, or maybe White Pongo in a last gesture of faith would point it out to them, hidden behind a portrait of Edgar Allan Poe, and then Walt and Rita Jane would emerge from that underground, heroic, hand in hand, ghost gone.

He could have drifted along with that thought, but he remembered Mr. Newfield instead. "Find that last reel of film!" They didn't want the audience to be waiting for the end. He turned from the pillar, the poster, and walked right into a solid White Pongo.

"Oh God!" Walt muttered but there was no escape.

The gorilla led him to a table and sat him down like a ragdoll. Across the table were piles of envelopes and stacks of leaflets and Walt knew what he was supposed to do. He had done this job before. After college, he got work stuffing envelopes. You would never have known in the basement of an ordinary looking house on a neighborhood street, a sort of factory was going on. Walt was a human machine. He created his own rhythm—right hand reach for the leaflet, fold, and left hand stuff the envelope and add it to the stack. That went on from the morning until the afternoon.

A couple weeks went by that way and then the work dried up. It was like a seasonal crop— the sun shined on the envelopes for a while, they bloomed and then they were all picked and gathered into cardboard boxes and shipped away. A sea that had been full of salmon was emptied out, leaving rivers nothing but water. Before that happened though—it may have been days or hours or only long minutes at the table—the point is, it didn't take Walt long to start sending out messages of help.

When the manager wasn't looking and when the manager's teenage son was in the other room, or off at school, Walt would write on the edges of those mailers he sent out. *Help! Being held prisoner by White Pongo!* or simply *Please rescue me*. Something along those lines. They were like messages in bottles thrown from the deck of a trawler. Who knew if anyone would get them? He could only hope.

There were probably fifty of them left in his wake before he finally got the nerve to leave the table and open the window. In the rush of cold air, Walt could look out and see a crowded street below. Marching bands, cowboys on horses, big balloon animals bobbing above the parade. Familiar cartoon characters lurched unsteadily in the winter air and with them appeared White Pongo, his giant rubber arms held out like a jumbo jet. It was freezing. Walt was falling and the only one who could catch him was a hundred foot helium gorilla.

For a moment, Walt thought he was on the floor of some Himalayan ice cave. He opened his eyes just enough to see their gloomy bedroom and he pulled a portion of the blanket back over him. That was better. That was all he needed and his eyes closed again.

He listened to the wind. The rain pelted the window and roof. He thought of the leak in the garage. There was also the kitchen faucet that was dripping and needed a new washer. Even a simple job like that, he didn't have the right tools for. The garage was a bigger problem. All the water running down the backyard hill through the ground seeped in the walls and made a shiny trickling stream. How many years had he been fighting that? Laying on thick coats of sealant with a paintbrush. He thought of the guy at the hardware store, a boar in a blue smock, who told Walt, "You can't stop running water. It goes where it wants to go. I've even seen it run uphill." This black hour wasn't a good time to think of all the jobs you needed to do and everything wrong in your life. Walt turned and glared at the clock. 2:39. That still gave him some room to sleep before the alarm.

He shut his eyes. The sound of wind and rain. His wife turned, then the bed became still again. Who could sleep with all this wind and rain and worrying? He would count sheep, but first he had to picture a place where the sun was shining, a meadow was green, where there were tangerine trees and marmalade skies.

"Are you going back to sleep?" the chickadee asked.

Walt nodded. He was so tired.

"Password?" the little bird said.

"What?" Walt wanted to say. Who needed
a password to sleep? The laughing chickadee
hopped on the branch in front of him as the
forest was filling in around him, strokes and
blurs of color coming into view. You didn't
need a password, or a button to press, you just
needed to want to be there.

The bird flew away as the rest of the world
appeared and Walt knew where he was.

This wasn't a lasting place, but it was beautiful. It reminded him of somewhere else he had
been. He remembered walking outside on the
first spring day when you could tell winter was
over, when the air felt squeezed like an orange,
damp and sweet. He remembered the sunny
shore of Lake Erie, the waves and sand, after all
those cold months. It was lovely there and he
thought of the long migration of people who
used to come here, riding ponies, families carrying a few belongings, staying for the warm
months, following the change of seasons back
and forth, staying only as long as they could.

Already, the woods around Walt were

beginning to dissolve. This peaceful waiting room was being replaced by a dream. The sky was showing through the branches, the trees were vanishing, all the lush green was turning into road, flat fields on either side of windows and the songs of birds became radio.

Walt didn't know much about baseball and he didn't know how he got to be the manager on a bus full of such men. He recognized the team name on the hats and shirts. Sometimes in the summer he would listen to the Tacoma Tigers play ball on the AM dial as he drove from town to town. It was entertaining, but he didn't know the players' names and he didn't know all the rules of the game. In no way was he capable of being their manager, but there he was. The bus lurched along the county road and Walt just had to accept it.

Fortunately, it wasn't for long. There was only so far he could go with that information. The team was gone, the bus was gone, but he was left in a baseball field. That much remained. It was dusk. The sky was turning pale purple above the line of thick blue trees. Across the wide empty field he saw fireflies and further up a couple bright stars.

It reminded him of those early summer

evenings when he had a bicycle. The day would cool into night and the houselights would come on. People on green porches dimly lit by lamps and laughing, telling stories, the cough that came from cigarettes. In the neighborhood calm when everyone was home and happy, he would ride along the sidewalks, simple as a kite.

On the grassy edge of the elementary school outfield, someone called out to him.

"Have you seen the tiger?" It was a couple with a flashlight. "You go that way," they told him, "and we'll go this way."

Walt didn't find out any more from them. Whoever they were, they ran off slopping light over the grass. Someone else yelped, shouted in the distance and a train horn moaned. The field was getting dark like a lake and something was floating across it.

"Is that the tiger?" Walt called. Where was everyone? Was that a tiger, and why was he chasing it? It moved like an animal, low and gray in the gloom, stopping and darting forward towards the end of the field where the woods grew. Walt was surprised he could move nearly as fast, his feet felt like a pinwheel. He could almost be flying above the ground. He used to pedal like that in dreams. Anytime the danger was too great, there was nowhere else to go but up. But he didn't dream about villains and monsters anymore. This was only a tiger.

He thought it would break into the cover of trees and then it would be free and lost from sight, but it didn't. That crazy tiger seemed to be having fun, running in the moonlight, leaping at moths and chasing fireflies. There was nothing to be afraid of, the tiger was only spinning around the night, growing up the trellis shaped bleacher seats and jumping off to the playground below.

Walt stepped off the unicycle he was riding again and rested it beside a jungle gym. He could hear a swing going back and forth. He could see the dark shape of someone or something slumping it and making it move. Walt got closer, walking through crickets as he neared the squeaking chain swing.

Walt used to ride his bike to this park on summer nights a long time ago. He would take a ride on those swings far enough that his feet could punch into the stars. He liked being back. But in all those years, he never saw a tiger.

There might have been one in forgotten games he used to play. When he was a boy, his imagination was filled with dinosaurs, robots and dangerous animals. His fuel was those old sci-fi and jungle movies he used to watch. They would take him to Mars or mysterious islands off Africa. He liked to climb the trees in the park and pretend he lived in them. Why wouldn't a tiger be up in those branches instead of on a swing?

It wasn't a tiger.

Walt was only ten feet away from the swing and he didn't have to wonder anymore.

The snowy fur was familiar but the size wasn't—the gorilla wasn't nearly as big as White Pongo. It wasn't Crash Corrigan underneath. Someone else, someone who preferred swings and playing in baseball fields at night was inside the gorilla suit.

Walt didn't mean to sneak up on him, he forgot how limited your sight was only looking out mask holes.

The swing gave a lurch and the ape almost fell off. Big fur-covered feet scuffed and caught the trampled ground and stopped the pendulum.

"Sorry," Walt said. "I startled you."

The white gorilla face stared at him and Walt could almost believe it was real. A young Pongo running off wild on a summer night the way Walt used to. When a shaggy arm reached up and removed the mask, Walt saw the boy's face.

"Air!" he gasped. "I can breathe again!"

It was a nice night. The crickets were threaded all through the dark and you could see the warm glow of the gas station over the trees.

"Do you know what time it is?" the boy said suddenly.

"No," Walt answered. He never wore a watch, he didn't need one.

The swing chirped nervously as the gorilla body hopped free. "I better get home. My dad will kill me."

"Is your dad Crash?"

The boy made a strange face for a gorilla. "Mr. Corrigan, I call him."

Walt said, "Oh." He didn't like to follow that thought.

"I have to hurry." The boy held the crumpled mask and turned. "I bet I'm late."

Walt didn't like the sound of the boy's voice when he asked, "Do you have a car?"

Walt remembered his car. It always appeared when he needed it, like a cowboy's trusty steed. An old Volkswagen Beetle waited for them. "This is how I know I'm in a dream.

I only have this car when I'm asleep." It was a fine, fun thing to drive around too, with a burbling engine, headlights glowing like owl eyes, dashboard dials trimmed with chrome. Sometimes Walt thought about buying one of these cars out in the real world, but why? This one was just as real when he was asleep. It made him think how strange it was to want anything when it was all just in your mind.

The Son of White Pongo gave Walt directions. They passed a telephone booth on a street corner, surrounded by so many moths attracted to its lonely yellow light that it looked like a rocket taking off. Quiet neighborhood streets with big leafy trees overhead, a moon chandelier, and the boy kept the car turning on Indian names: a left on Seneca Ave, down Shawnee, onto Tecumseh Place.

"There's my house," said the boy.

The Volkswagen purred into the driveway. In the big front window, you could see a TV. A Western was on…a circle of covered wagons, campfire and starlight, a black and white desert and in all that peaceful beauty, a cowboy listening for danger. Walt supposed Crash watched a lot of those shows. He might even be in this one.

The boy hopped out of the car and said, "I better go in the back door, I might be able to sneak in. Thanks for the ride, mister." With his mask back on, he looked like a gorilla again.

"Good luck."

The cowboy on that big living room TV heard something. His eyes narrowed on a noise out in the sagebrush.

"Oh God," Walt muttered and then the cowboy looked straight into the camera, right at the little German car buzzing in his driveway.

"Oh no!" Walt jammed the gearshift into reverse and gunned the Beetle onto the shadowy street. Popping into first gear, he caught a glimpse of the Corrigan ranch house just as a horse leaped over the backyard fence with a cowboy waving a gun from that height.

It was a mad chase, exactly what you would expect from Republic Pictures. All it lacked was the orchestra background, or maybe Walt just didn't hear that over the clopping hooves on tar and his dream car pitching and braking and taking corners in a blur. There wasn't much hope of losing the cowboy in this neighborhood. Walt needed the open road where he could release the 40 horsepower engine and escape. A glimpse in the rear view mirror showed an albino ape on horseback riding after him. The next moment it was Crash in his Western clothes, whirling his lasso, looping it like a helicopter blade large enough to catch a car. In despair, Walt pictured the highway and he was there. Sometimes that's all you have to do and it works.

Other cars rolled along with him in some hurry to somewhere. No sign of the horse rider, but Walt didn't want to think of him—that might make him appear.

The road curved around the big hills of town, carved through what used to be a green valley with trees and streams. Lots of houses, signs, stores and traffic on either side of him. When he was a kid he used to dream King Kong could emerge from behind the treetop hills. The ground would be shaking and the town swept into smoke as everyone ran. Those Saturday movies they played on TV with jungles and monsters and haunted worlds made a big impression on Walt. That was probably where he first saw White Pongo too, back when television was mysterious, waiting for The Count Misfit Show on a late Friday night.

There was no King Kong now—he hadn't had those dreams in years—but as the traffic crawled around another bend, he thought of White Pongo. The highway passed beside the Museum of History and Industry. This was the same route his school bus used to travel and he remembered the way everyone would hush as they went by. In the basement of that museum, at the end of the hall, there was a water fountain and a glass display case. Every kid on the bus would be thinking of that exhibit practically hidden away from sight in the gloom. A glass wall not much larger than a telephone booth was where White Pongo stood looking out. A plaque by the rail told the story that led him to this deserted spot.

Captured in Africa by a gorilla hunter who shot White Pongo's parents, he was brought to America as a baby and bought by a family who raised him like their son. People used to stop their cars on the street to watch the family eat dinner and play games. As the gorilla grew, he got bigger and stronger and pretty soon he was swinging from the ceiling, breaking furniture. When he crushed the piano like an accordion, they knew if they didn't bring him to a zoo there would be nothing left of their house. How awful to think of that poor gorilla, no bigger than a school child, wearing a blue suit and hat, being led into that concrete room and pried away from the family he knew. He would sit by the window all those years and watch for them to come back.

It is understandable that a chap who can bend iron bars and stretch truck tires as if they were rubber bands might be unimpressed by the accomplishments of puny humans. While we race like schizophrenic squirrels in a revolving cage filled with status symbols, time clocks, tax forms and parking meters, he relaxes in uncluttered, air-conditioned comfort and reigns in quiet majesty as king of Woodland Park Zoo.

—Tom Robbins from "Bobo and His Keeper"

After the famous ape died, he was stuffed like a shot deer and stuck behind glass in a ferocious pose, as if he was just ripping through those plastic jungle plants, about to take a swipe at you. As soon as the museum moved safely out of the school bus sight, behind billboards and Safeway trucks, they would all start talking again and laughing with crumpled wrappers thrown from seat to seat.

Walt told his kids about White Pongo and wanted to show them that white gorilla taxidermy down in the museum basement, but so much has changed. When they went there it was no longer on display. The lady at the gift shop counter couldn't say where White Pongo had gone.

Maybe he was in storage? If Walt closed his eyes, he could see that White Pongo and all the other childhood ghosts had slipped into a hazy museum of memories.

He couldn't close his eyes though, he was driving with all those other cars, past familiar sights and new things built over places he used to know. Even the maps in dreams would be different each night, nothing could stay the same. How could it, anywhere? What once was, had to make way. That was true for a gorilla, the actor in disguise, or the B-movie can of film their world existed in.

He was near the school, still on the old bus route, and he recognized trees and sidewalks.

When he was in elementary school, he would look out the bus window and imagine he was a tiny pilot and the plane could jet along the street, no bigger than a dragonfly, in and out of irrigation pipes, around and over any obstacle. It would land in the lot where the buses pulled in to curb in a long yellow row. The plane would hide camouflaged in the leaves like an angel waiting for him to be done with school for the day.

Walt didn't return too often to the school. There were only a few things that would make him go back, that still rattled like a couple old marbles in a cup. A few things that had turned hard and dried and some other things had never stopped being flowers.

If he parked his car and went inside, he would go over that wax finished floor, past the lockers and classroom doors and papered walls, to the gumball machine at the end of the hall. It was the kind they had at supermarkets, a metal stand with a glass helmet on and filled with baubles. You put a quarter in and out would come a prize. But these weren't candies and plastic toys. A parent, someone like Walt, or a teacher, a custodian—whoever had some prayer to give—would stop at the machine. After the bell rang and the hallways were full of boys and girls, someone young would turn the dial and catch it, falling into their hand.

Walt tried to help. He could remember those school days and he could turn those feelings into something shiny, fit in a bauble that might give comfort if the right person found it. That was the hope anyway. Like alchemy, you try to make things get better.

Why imagine the sort of world they're being

taught to see?

What did they have to look forward to? The country was still in an endless Orwell war, the so-called president was a warning right out of their American history textbooks. Their very planet was getting crushed by violence, poison and human greed. It kept Walt up worrying at night. Education had to be more than the practice of getting out of bed early, training to go be closed inside all day like an adult at an office job. What they were learning in school was what they would bring out into the world.

Oh, and that made him think of the letter they got from their son's teacher:

Dear Parents,
We are working on a dystopian project for class. Students are required to create in writing, visual arts or music, a Dystopian world. The assignment will be due Monday.

His wife wrote a letter back:

I am curious about this assignment. I know you have a plan for these kids. I am just wondering about this. I know these children have grown up learning hard facts about the loss of species, greenhouse gasses, toxicity, and more recently the loss of human rights and honest leadership. I often wonder how the inevitable emotions around these things effect young people.

I wonder about asking them to visualize in detail a dystopian future. I so wish they were visualizing a positive future. I trust your skill as a teacher of young minds. I just write out of curiosity. Do you think writing and reading about dystopias as one unfolds in reality helps them to express fears or anxieties? Or perhaps gives form to despair? Or is it just a literary idea?

Then the teacher wrote back:

I believe the benefit of envisioning dystopian so-cieties is not to dwell on the negative aspects of failing humanity/civilization, but instead to focus on the contrast of what change could enable or fix desperately negative societies into the ones we need. By looking at frighteningly bad situations, we hope to foster a drive to pursue that which gives life and develops growth; especially with how much negativity is in the world presently—allow-ing teens to channel those negative thoughts and explore their own perspectives into a fictionalized world. This also provides a space to ponder and re-flect on what things could be like. I'm discovering that students are developing characters that take matters into their own hands, find a voice amidst the chaos, and make a desperate change in their communities for the greater good—while others, to be quite frank, are just tapping into the ability to write creative and outrageous stories. I'm happy with both levels of investment and motivation!

Furthermore, dystopian texts are the latest/revis-ited genre which most teens are consuming at a rapid pace—so allowing them to partake in this via writing their own narrative—will provide the opportunity to practice fictional creative writing skills that builds nicely off of familiar tropes and format, while fostering belonging as a writer in this style.

I hope this answers some of your questions!

She wrote one last time, and it was like the phenomenon of dreams or movies too the way Walt could hear her voice, "I think it's because dystopian stories are such big sellers in their age group, you are trying to engage them. But I think they are so popular because it's all they are publishing! So what else is there? It's a monster that feeds itself." And she told him even she got overwhelmed with negativity and she hoped the kids would get a balance with more positive information too.

The teacher replied, "We hope to foster a drive to pursue that which gives life and develop growth." But it meant an awful lot of hope.

Walt wanted to fit something more in a bauble than those assignments he did in school. Where were they now? They had turned to dust. If they were lucky, maybe something grew from one, like wildflowers…or a river, or a tree.

Walt left the school. The heavy door clanked

shut behind him, and he didn't need his car. Not where he now found himself…on the long metal deck of a ship far out at sea.

It was either some time at night, or very early morning. The sky, water, the skin of the ship, everything was blue. The breeze was probably blue if you could see it, painting it all. The engine rumbled and an orchestra of tin cans seemed to rattle beneath. The rigging wires up to the aerials sung like harp strings. There was a lot of noise on this vibrating freighter, bolted to the waves.

In a clearing before him, Walt saw the gorilla's bamboo cage standing alone. The pale moon-colored creature inside was slumped against the bars. This was how the movie *White Pongo* ended, the ape with the bullets still in it, trapped and on its way to England. It wasn't a happy ending for the beast and anyone with a heart would have wanted better. But anyone walking out of the theater in 1945 would have to wait 73 years for the action to resume.

White Pongo's snarling face turned towards Walt as he approached. Walt wasn't afraid—that was just the creature's look. It was worn like a mask. As Walt flipped a bucket over to sit on, the face regarded him.

THE SKULL OF WHITE PONGO

Description:

Lot 767. WHITE PONGO GORILLA HEAD GEAR WORN BY RAY "CRASH" COR-RIGAN. (P.R.C. Pictures, 1945) Mecha-nized gorilla head piece armature measur-ing 9 x 14 inches. Constructed of metal, leather, resin and wax. Screen-worn by legendary gorilla actor and specialist Ray "Crash" Corrigan. The armature consists of a headband and sidebars attached to up-per and lower jaw pieces. The jaw pieces are fashioned of wax with resin teeth and gums affixed. Upper and lower plates are wired and operated independently to open and close the mouth of what would have been the overlaying gorilla mask's rubber skin. There are two small plated levers that rest on the side of the actor's face to affect the Gorilla's snarl. Formerly from the collection of Forrest J Ackerman. In vintage very good condition. Minor rust marks. **$3,000 - $5,000**

Walt didn't know if he had actually stepped into the black and white movie. It felt that way. He had to treat it as if this was real. Of course, he would be someone sympathetic to the captured gorilla.

Maybe he had a harmonica in his pocket? He would play songs to cheer up Pongo. Or maybe he brought fresh fruit and vegetables from the galley and a bond was formed between the ape and the lonesome sailor. Somehow though, Walt knew that wasn't quite true. Under the cover of all this blue, he was a stowaway and this was his only time to safely creep out of his hiding place and get some air. The fact that there was a gorilla on deck gave him someone to talk to. Walt stored up a lot of words during a long day hiding and he was glad he had this companion who was in a way just as trapped as him.

"Hello again," Walt said. He stayed in the shadow of the big trumpet shaped air vent. "How was your day?"

The gorilla made a noise like a sigh and said, "Listen friend, before you start talking again, do you have a cigarette?"

Walt almost fell off the bucket.

Ray spent his free time in early 1934 studying the mannerisms of larger primates at the San Diego Zoo. Shortly thereafter, Ray Corrigan was encased in the hot and stifling interior of one of his five expensive, handmade gorilla suits, aping his way through classic Hollywood features.

—from The World's Most Famous Movie Ranch: The Story of Ray "Crash" Corrigan and Corrig- anville

White Pongo reached two furry arms upwards and removed his mask. Crash took a deep breath and exhaled gratefully. "What a day…" He rubbed the back of his neck with his rubber glove then held that hand out to Walt. "How about that cigarette?"

Walt patted his pockets and was surprised to find a crumpled pack of Lucky Strikes. That was Jack Benny's sponsor, he remembered. He expected the radio voice of Don Wilson to explain, "Lucky's fine tobacco picks you up when you're low, calms you down when you're tense, puts you on the right level to feel and do your level best." Walt handed the pack to Crash. "You can keep it."

"Thanks."

Walt watched Crash pick at the cigarettes with a giant rubber hand, deftly, like an ape surgeon, removing one from the cellophane and paper. Crash popped it in the corner of his mouth and asked, "You got a match?"

"Oh." Walt checked his pockets again. Some car keys, a dollar, a piece of folded paper and a pen. He also had a round, smooth lucky stone. It reminded him of the moon.

"Really?" said Crash in a huff. "No matches?"

"Well…" Walt was going to joke something about how gorillas haven't discovered fire yet, when a steel door plunged open, throwing bright light on them. Walt shielded his eyes and Crash quickly ducked back into his mask.

"There he is!" someone shouted. "The stowaway!"

Through his fingers, Walt could see the crew spill out onto the deck. They quickly surrounded him and someone lifted him off the bucket and someone else shook him, face close, creased with shadows.

"You know what we do with stowaways out

on the high seas?"

Walt could guess.

He had a pretty good idea.

He had read Jack London and Robert Louis Stevenson and seen movies like this.

He hoped he was wrong.

But he wasn't.

They dragged him to the side of the ship and pushed his back against the cold steel. "We throw them overboard!" the face snarled.

"That's what I figured," said Walt. It would have been the perfect time for White Pongo to go berserk and break through the bamboo bars, but that didn't happen. Up and over Walt went.

He wanted to turn the channel. If only he could. He was in some unbalanced falling tangle, the sound of the sea creasing around the hull, blue sky, blue water, and blue ship chugging away. The sound engineer added the cry of a seagull, but that might have been a mistake. Wouldn't that mean they weren't far from land?

Walt was waiting for the ocean to swallow him, for the cold shock of drowning, sinking and becoming lost in the food chain. Instead, he landed on his back, on something soft as a bed.

When he moved, the mattress beneath him

gave and rippled. Sitting up, he saw that he was at rest on a widespread lily pad made of garbage. Millions of plastic pieces formed a Sargasso Sea.

The freighter had steamed right through. A tiny light, no bigger than a star. It left and took the rumble of its engine into the blue night, or early morning, it was hard to tell. Its wake was already covered over with bottles, fishing net, plastic bags, wrappers, crumpled containers, clocks, packaging and toys, tires and floating junk. The flotsam was so thick Walt could get to his feet and walk on it.

He was on an island the size of the city dump. That's why he heard that seagull—it probably lived here. There were other gulls too, here and there showing up like lightbulbs. They had food and shelter, with nests tucked among the plastic and rubber and bluebottle flies. They could be a thousand miles from land, it didn't matter. Walt knew he was as good as shipwrecked.

Still no sign of a sun or moon in the blue sky. It was dark, but something caught his eye in the swaying piles of garbage at his feet. He reached past what looked like the workings of a typewriter and pulled a glass bottle free.

He guessed this would be his life now, picking among the ruins.

He thought the bottle might be one he wrote a message in—wouldn't that be funny if it was? *Help! Being held prisoner by White Pongo!* At this point, being thrown off a ship and marooned, he could use a little humor. He brushed the debris off the glass and took a look.

There was enough pale dawn light coming from the horizon to see there wasn't a note circled inside. He held the bottle up flat to that horizon glow and he could tell what it held. A little ship was inside, a perfectly made replica of the barge they had their radio station on. It had the antenna sprouting from it like a tall mast, with a dot of red light blinking at the top. Walt could even hear faint music coming from it.

As he inspected it, it looked real enough to really be anchored against the horizon line. He could have been holding that bottle like binoculars, staring at the black ship, its portholes sparkling, the new day sunshine glinting on it and a few gulls circling that crooked broadcasting antenna. As if entranced all along by some magic illusion, when he lowered the bottle, the ship was no longer trapped in it. It floated upon the water not far away. Birds wheeled about it in the air, lifted by those high lonesome kilowatts emanating from ship to shore.

"Say!" a voice called Walt from nearby. Only a holler away sat Gene Autry atop his horse, Champion. "We have to hurry if we're going to make that next broadcast!" Another horse stood beside him, riderless.

Walt ran across the blanket of trash, right over the sleeping back of a rusted DeSoto sedan, knocking tin cans and a xylophone out of his way. He couldn't recall ever riding a horse but he didn't let Gene down. With a leap, he saddled up and they were on their way.

A note pinned to the saddle rattled in the breeze:

GENE AUTRY'S COWBOY CODE

1. The Cowboy must never shoot first, hit a smaller man, or take unfair advantage.
2. He must never go back on his word, or a trust confided in him.
3. He must always tell the truth.
4. He must be gentle with children, the elderly, and animals.
5. He must not advocate or possess racially or religiously intolerant ideas.
6. He must help people in distress.
7. He must be a good worker.
8. He must keep himself clean in thought, speech, action, and personal habits.
9. He must respect women, parents, and his nation's laws.
10. The Cowboy is a patriot.

Gene Autry made it look easy, like it was every other day he rode a horse on top the water, jumping from patch to floating patch, towards a barge that was broadcasting cowboy radio.

Walt followed close behind. He could see the green, deep riffled water when the horse leaped to the next plastic landing. He knew he wasn't in any danger. If anything, it felt like he had gone back in time, to put a dime in the plastic rocking horse ride in front of Food Giant. He used to pretend this very thing back then, sing-song galloping along over prairies and canyons in imagination.

His horse flew like Pegasus and he could see seals below him, beds of kelp that turned back into the roots holding the next floating island they landed on.

Champion took Gene in a leap onto the deck of the radio ship. It was amazing to watch, like a calligraphy brush stroke. If Walt could have duplicated that he would, but he had to hold on tight as his horse shied and slid on the rubble next to the hull.

He saw the way up. A cement stairway with a handrail scuffed by skateboard grinding. Walt ran up the steps. He didn't know how late he was. He knew he had dreams where he was late to work and it felt like this. So many weird worries.

He thought of the birds. Were they wor-ried, sitting on trees and singing all day? Why did people make it so hard on themselves? Was there a short-circuit fault in reincarnation— were people forgetting the lessons they learned every life?

He pictured the lilac tree that grew behind their house. Every winter it turned into bare branches like deer antlers sprouting from the cold ground. Then every spring, the leaves and birds would reappear. Wasn't that a miracle? A tree that remembered how to grow every time it went away.

Walt ran up the steps. Beside the door, stuck in the middle of the brick wall, was a flat gray stone reading: "1949. Golden Anniversary."

It made him think of the world at that time,

still recovering from an awful war. And poor White Pongo out there peddling balm in a film can.

Through the glass door, he could see into his office. The lights were on and his boss was in there already.

At least Walt didn't have to clock in. He remembered his first job in high school when he had to stamp a card every time he arrived and left. That would make anyone nervous.

Things in the office were busy already. He had work waiting for him. There were messages scattered about his desk and from the pneumatic tube above, another capsule fell and joined the pile scattered on the tabletop and floor. It looked like a submarine graveyard. He picked up the latest one, still moving, for the discussion already in progress. Now he could read them like telegrams from a sinking steamship.

Dear Studio Committee,

This is not a purchase that can be decided by a vote. It is a fee-related question. I have consulted with the Budget Planning Analyst about the purchase of seminar room tuffets from studio fees and he was not in favor: tuffets are supposed to be part and parcel of what is covered by tuition, along with any other basic material, such as tables, desks, lights in the room, etc., PLUS salaries. When we purchased tuffets for the Pongorium, that was supposed to be a one-time deal, and that is slightly different, given that it is a shared space and a specialized space, as a critique room, which one could use as an argument for specialized tuffets.

The Budget Planning Analyst suggests that we could probably rationalize covering half the cost of the tuffets from those fees, as these tuffets will be valued by art students over and above the regularly supplied tuffets. The other half would have to come from our operating budgets. If you all would like to pool your Studio budgets and cover the rest of the cost, the tuffets can conceivably be purchased. Walt can run the figures on that.

Please let me know if you have any other questions.

Thanks,
Sam Newfield
Director

No sooner had Walt finished reading when another message dropped to his desktop.

Sam,

First, I want to thank you for all your help with clarification regarding the use of fee account monies. As you know, I agree with the committee on the vote that we took during a recent meeting, and the decision to distribute the money to benefit our artists as directly as possible by purchasing tuffets for the seminar room.

Many thanks.

—Algar

Walt rubbed his eyes. "What's a tuffet?"

The little bird who invited him in and out of dreams told him the dictionary definition, "A tuffet, pouffe, or hassock is a piece of furniture used as a footstool or low seat."

Walt was struck by another falling tube before he could respond.

We never discussed this in a meeting. Last week when I learned we were investing fees into the seminar room for tuffets, I rescheduled my Gorilla Limnology class to take place in that room. I think the argument can be made that we need that room every quarter. If we are expanding its common use to include my class among others, regardless of who is teaching, I think the argument for using fees for the specialized tuffets is stronger.

—Clio

It only took a moment for Algar's reply.

By now, Walt didn't have to read the messages anymore; he could hear their voices like a shelf of competing radios.

occasion. If I did not, there would have been none of either in the production studio. I cannot ever remember a time when I was offered an opportunity to purchase new "furniture" by any other means—and I have been here for 20 years.

It came to a critical state in my studio space when I realized that I was going to have to instruct a group of 20 artists and I only had two suitable tuffets. The rest were crude stools, or completely ripped up tuffets with stuffing coming out of them. I had to "borrow" tuffets from wherever I could.

The purchase of tuffets for the Pongorium was also a wake-up call as all the tuffets in there were a terrible mismatch of broken up disrepair, and old butcher block construction. When I was Interim Director, I was going through the building with the studio Chairman and President. I was instructed by the Chairman to "not complain about our space." But the main comment I remember was the President saying upon our exit from the Pongorium, "You really need some new tuffets in here."

—Renault

The canisters kept dropping loud and clear, hitting the tabletop like teapots. He caught one and unsealed it. It was Algar again and he was fuming.

Sam & Co,

As you know the seminar room is NOT AN OPEN CLASSROOM. It is part of the stationary motions lab. Like any of the other studio facilities—it is specifically designed to fulfill the needs of artists enrolled under MY instruction. Can we use the Animal Textures Lab for Jungle Climatology Studies?

So, after further consideration—and knowing that the seminar room is high use—I'm withdrawing my offer to share the space.

As it is no longer to be used, I will need a classroom to teach Primate Motion in the fall.

—Algar

The air was flooded with clashing radio signals. It was severe interference. No doubt about it, Walt was back at work. There were no cowboys or great apes to save him.

Sam,

I am surprised by this decision which overrides the committee on how these fees are used. Especially, since there is a precedent of purchasing tuffets for the Pongorium with no apparent similar scrutiny. Does this imply that the studio is misusing fees? The tuffet purchase in particular opened up the possibility of having to find another room to use for Primate Motion and it appeared to the entire studio faculty that this use of fees falls under the purview of their intended use. If it truly is the case that tuition pays for chairs, tables, lights, in the rooms, etc., why isn't this happening? Our facility is falling apart and every studio classroom needs to be upgraded. Like the Pongorium tuffet purchase, this was our attempt to be proactive and start a process of improving our facilities.

Thanks
Wayne

Walt had been witness to other conversations like this—when the new office manager was hired, they were mad that his office was bigger than some of theirs. Not to mention his tuffet. Sometimes the studio was a clubhouse, a treehouse with the rope ladder pulled up and squabbling in the leaves.

Sam's response clattered onto the desk and his voice broke out.

Wayne,

There are plenty of tuffets available in surplus, but perhaps not of the luxurious quality we all would prefer. If the tuffet situation is that dire, I recommend that option be pursued, and that should be at no cost to the department.

That would be a first step.

I appreciate the idea of being proactive, but it's unlikely that $200 tuffets will be approved.

We will not get into an internal battle for space. I hasten to remind you, as will our Budget

Walt was tossing and turning. This had become a real nightmare and he didn't seem to be aware of how to stop it. He was stuck in it. He wanted to wake up, but he also wished he could keep sleeping—but finding a door to a different dream wasn't happening yet.

current director. After all, his track record is not good. It took five years to fulfill a request for a standard Bell & Howell Autoload projector for the seminar room!

Furthermore, the seminar room cannot be expected to share the facility, and then pay for its maintenance and upkeep! The tuffets are only the tip of the iceberg.

Have a great weekend!

—Algar

For a long time before, Walt wished he could be part of an artistic utopia—creative people with a creative vision—he still wished that could happen, but the exchanges that came through the pneumatic tubes in rapid succession gave him doubt. If this was any example, it didn't look like artists would ever be able to lead a society. No wonder, the way they behaved, arguing over tuffets!

It was so distressing he woke up. Why was he wasting precious dreamtime on his job?

He understood as he got out of bed.

It was just his body conjuring a nightmare so he would go downstairs to the bathroom. It worked too. There was no way he wanted to stay in that dream.

When he returned to bed, Walt pulled a blanket around his shoulder. He forgot to look at the clock. He didn't know how much time was left. He couldn't reset his mental clock; he would have to rely on the alarm.

It must be getting close to dawn though. Walt heard a bird and followed it to sleep.

He was walking in the neighborhood where he used to live. The old cars were parked along the street. The grass by the sidewalk was long, it hadn't been cut and dandelions poked through. Houses, gardens, trees—he spent a lot of time walking around these blocks, knowing things like a crow.

One of those things was a big bone padlocked to a tree.

It wasn't far from the sidewalk, only a few steps across the lawn. The little green house at the back of the yard didn't seem to mind. In fact, the sign made it clear that they wanted you to stop and look and be aware. The sign was tapped into the ground like a vampire stake and painted on the wood were the words:

MASTODON VERTEBRA
FOUND IN ALASKA, 1972

It was a huge round wheel of bone slab with a chain that ran through the hole in the middle, looping it to a flowering cherry tree. The ends of the chain were padlocked together. Big as it was, this was the smallest piece of a beast that once walked along in the Ice Age. Walt could imagine the rest of the mastodon linked invisibly to that bone.

Something similar happened to the skull of White Pongo.

After sixteen years captivity in the zoo, when White Pongo died, the whole city was sad. Nobody knew why he died young. His body went to the museum for an autopsy and to taxidermy it for display. Physicians, scientists, reporters, professors and students came and went from the room. Somewhere in that traffic, White Pongo's skull disappeared from the cold storage vault where his skeleton was being stored. A headless gorilla haunted the shadows of the museum and the rainy morning windows were streaked by its fingers as it wandered the halls.

That continued for thirty years, like a gothic jungle movie, until one evening a box appeared on the steps of the museum. Inside was a skull with the words White Pongo penciled on. For that poor gorilla, it was just more of a lifetime of being lost and found again.

Like the time Walt found a roll of film at the Goodwill. It was in a slim cardboard box on a stack of used books. A ferocious white gorilla was pictured on the lid and Walt had no doubt White Pongo was on the plastic spool of Super-8 inside.

With that treasure on the seat beside him, he drove the VW to the movie theater.

—from *White Pongo*

Walt parked in the lot by the sandstone hill and left his trusty car for the next time he would need it. There were days in the waking world when he almost felt the car was real, waiting for him to slide into. But there were no objects in dreams that could transfer into day; they were made of moonlight and breeze. Dreams were only real when you were in them.

"Where have you been?" Sam Newfield called from the side door. "We need that last roll of film!"

Walt hurried. "Don't worry." He held the box up in the air. "I've got it."

The manager held the door open. "Then get it to the projection booth! Quick!"

"Yes sir." He felt the spirit of Gene Autry running to the Radio Ranch. There was never a moment to lose when the song had to be heard, or all that you loved would be gone. You wouldn't want all the green grassland, orchard, farm and gardens and pastures turned into tar, concrete, useless stores, duplexes, electric wires tying up the sky. In *The Phantom Empire*, Gene was always one step ahead of the nightmare. Even Crash Corrigan, at the end of his days, had his trailer, his backyard sunlight, bright clean Western colors drying on the wash line, ready to wear. He could rest his boots up on the rail and watch the big sky.

And while Walt climbed the steep dark stairs to the projectionist, he could hear the scratchy sound of the ancient timeworn film coming from the screen below. The singing cowboy was telling everyone, "Radio Ranch signing off, wishing you all happiness and good luck."

The edges were getting fuzzy, the picture flecked with blots and streaks, as Walt turned his attention and knocked on the door.

Seeing the projectionist was always a surprise—he looked just like Mark Twain, white suit rumpled with creases like waves, and the narrow room was crammed like a submarine. Cranks and levers and gears and the crackle light of morning electricity. An ancient projection machine turned and toiled like Rumpelstiltskin, rattling, flickering, steam driven as the silver pouring propellers of Captain Nemo churning up the harbor, starting the seagulls, stirring the seaweed and waking the seals.

Also, pushed in the corner of the crowded projection booth stood the Transforming Machine. Walt had seen it many times since childhood, forgotten it and remembered it again.

The last roll of film was spinning, the dream world would keep running without him and Walt knew it was time for him to leave now. He would be back again. Everything would be waiting.

The Mark Twain projectionist left the spilling light of his station and took Walt by the sleeve. He was easy to lead.

With a wry laugh, the famous author lifted

the newspaper off a nearby stool and gave it a wave. The headlines read:

WALT AMHERST IS AWAKE

First of all, Walt thought, how can that be a headline? Then he decided it meant he must be asleep.

"There's no need for alarm," said Mark Twain, "the transforming ray will not harm you, but merely take the memory of this place away." He opened the glass door and Walt stepped behind it.

Steam hissed around his feet, cracking sparks, smoke and lightning. Walt put his hands on the window, but there was nothing to hold onto—he was leaving, going into a cloud and there was nothing to see anymore.

The projection room was gone. Wherever he was happened a long time ago, like another life. For a second, Walt could almost remember it, as he reached across to turn off the sound of the alarm clock waking him up.

WALT AMHERST IS AWAKE
Written by Allen Frost
January—April 2018

Books by Good Deed Rain

Saint Lemonade, Allen Frost, 2014. Two novels illustrated by the author in the manner of the old Big Little Books.

Playground, Allen Frost, 2014. Poems collected from seven years of chapbooks.

Roosevelt, Allen Frost, 2015. A Pacific Northwest novel set in July, 1942, when a boy and a girl search for a missing elephant. Illustrated throughout by Fred Sodt.

5 Novels, Allen Frost, 2015. Novels written over five years, featuring circus giants, clockwork animals, detectives and time travelers.

The Sylvan Moore Show, Allen Frost, 2015. A short story omnibus of 193 stories written over 30 years.

www.ingramcontent.com/pod-product-compliance
Lightning Source LLC
Chambersburg PA
CBHW050148110726
47898CB00008B/2720

Town in a Cloud, Allen Frost, 2015. A 3 part book of poetry, written during the Bellingham rainy seasons of fall, winter, and spring.

A Flutter of Birds Passing Through Heaven: A Tribute to Robert Sund. 2016. Edited by Allen Frost and Paul Piper. The story of a legendary Ish River poet & artist.

At the Edge of America, Allen Frost, 2016. Two novels in one book blend time travel in a mythical poetic America.

Lake Erie Submarine, Allen Frost, 2016. A two week vacation in Ohio inspired these poems, illustrated by the author.

and Light, Paul Piper, 2016. Poetry written over three years. Illustrated with watercolors by Penny Piper.

The Book of Ticks, Allen Frost, 2017. A giant collection of 8 mysterious adventures featuring Phil Ticks. Illustrated throughout by Aaron Gunderson.

I Can Only Imagine, Allen Frost, 2017. Five adventures of love and heartbreak dreamed in an imaginary world. Cover & color illustrations by Annabelle Barrett.

The Orphanage of Abandoned Teenagers, Allen Frost, 2017. A fictional guide for teens and their parents. Illustrated by the author.

In the Valley of Mystic Light: An Oral History of the Skagit Valley Arts Scene, 2017. Edited by Claire Swedberg & Rita Hupy.

Different Planet, Allen Frost, 2017. Four science fiction adventures: reincarnation, robots, talking animals, outer space and clones. Cover & illustrations by Laura Vasyutynska.

Go with the Flow: A Tribute to Clyde Sanborn. 2018. Edited by Allen Frost. The life and art of a timeless river poet.

Homeless Sutra, Allen Frost, 2018. Four stories: Sylvan Moore, a flying monk, a water salesman, and a guardian rabbit.

The Lake Walker, Allen Frost 2018. A little novel set in black and white like one of those old European movies about death and life.

A Hundred Dreams Ago, Allen Frost, 2018. A winter book of poetry and prose. Illustrated by Aaron Gunderson.

Almost Animals, Allen Frost, 2018. A collection of linked stories, thinking about what makes us animals.

The Robotic Age, Allen Frost, 2018. A vaudeville magician and his robot track down ghosts. Illustrated throughout by Aaron Gunderson.

Kennedy, Allen Frost, 2018. This sequel to Roosevelt is a coming-of-age fable set during two weeks in 1962 in a mythical Kennedy-land. Illustrated throughout by Fred Sodt.

Fable, Allen Frost, 2018. There's something going on in this country and I can best relate it in fable: the parable of the rabbits, a bedtime story, and the diary of our trip to Ohio.

Elbows & Knees: Essays & Plays, Allen Frost, 2018. A thrilling collection of writing about some of my favorite subjects, from B-movies to Brautigan.

The Last Paper Stars, Allen Frost, 2019. A trip back in time to the 20 year old mind of Frankenstein, and two other worlds of the future.

Walt Amherst is Awake, Allen Frost, 2019. The dreamworld of an office worker. Illustrated by Aaron Gunderson.

Good Deed Rain author & publisher